CDC

40p

Mills & Boon

BEST SELLER ROMANCE

A chance to read and collect some of the best-loved novels from
Mills & Boon—the world's largest publisher of romantic fiction.

Every month, two titles by favourite Mills & Boon authors will
be republished in the *Best Seller Romance* series.

GW00371666

Sally Wentworth

JILTED

MILLS & BOON LIMITED
ETON HOUSE   18–24 PARADISE ROAD
RICHMOND   SURREY TW9 ISR

First published in Great Britain 1983 by Mills & Boon Limited

© Sally Wentworth 1983

Australian copyright 1983 Philippine copyright 1983 Reprinted 1983 This edition 1989

ISBN 0 263 76393 5

Set in Monophoto Plantin 10 on 11½ pt 02–8904–56040

Made and printed in Great Britain

CHAPTER ONE

ALEXANDRA CURTIS stood among the large congregation and watched the man she loved being married to one of her oldest friends. The sun shone through the arched windows of the old church, but, mercifully, it was difficult to see her face clearly because she was near a pillar supporting the carved roof and was covered by its deep shadow. That people were looking at her in surreptitious curiosity, she knew; she could feel their eyes boring into her back, wondering, surmising, see the heads turned to look at her and then quickly, almost guiltily, away. But her own eyes she kept fixed steadily on the prayer book in her hand, her face set into a tight mask that betrayed not even a flicker of emotion.

The bride's voice was so soft that you could hardly hear it, but the bridegroom made his responses in a firm, clear tone that echoed round the walls of the ancient building. Alexa gripped the book until her knuckles showed white, staring down at it blindly. But then she forced herself to look up and watch as the best man handed over the ring and the groom slipped it on to the finger of his bride. She tried not to look at his face as he did so, but some masochistic dictate compelled her to. A sharp stab of pain ran through her as she saw the look of love and pride on his face, a look that had once been hers alone.

Now it was over, they were officially man and wife. The congregation were singing another hymn while the bridal party filed into the vestry to sign the register. They seemed to be gone for a very long time. The wait started to become intolerable as people began to talk to one another, their heads close together and their voices lowered to almost a whisper. That several of them were talking about her, Alexa could tell from the over-casual way they glanced in her direction. Bitterness filled her and for a moment she wished fervently that she hadn't come to the wedding. But pride had forced her to attend, that and the knowledge of the cruel gossip that would arise if she didn't. Although people would be bound to gossip anyway, she realised with a sudden feeling of sick helplessness; it wasn't every day that a man jilted his fiancée and married her oldest friend instead, the one she'd chosen to be her bridesmaid.

The vicar came out of the vestry and signalled to the organist, who began to play a triumphal wedding march as the bridal procession reformed and moved slowly down the aisle towards her. Elaine, the new Mrs Mark Kelsey, looked radiantly happy, smiling at everyone, her hand on her husband's arm. When she saw Alexa the smile slipped a little, but then was quickly back in place as her eyes moved on to other, safer faces.

There was a long delay outside the church as photographs were taken, every conceivable combination of bride and groom, best man, bridesmaids, bride's family, groom's family, and then of course there was the group photograph. Alexa made sure she was at the back, hidden behind a tall man so that only the brim of her straw hat, with its gay pink flowers, was visible. A vintage white Rolls-Royce picked up the bridal couple to take them the short distance to the hotel where the reception was being held, while the guests squeezed into the line of wedding cars.

The worst part of living in a small town is that everyone knows everyone else, especially if you've been born and brought up there too. Alexa's family had lived in Seabrook for three generations, beginning way back when her grandfather had come there as a young doctor and had set up a practice which her father had eventually taken over and had run until both her parents had been killed in a car smash while they were on holiday in America a little under three years ago. As Alexa was their only child it had come as a very terrible blow, but she was nineteen then and so legally of age. The house, of course, had to be sold, and at first she'd thought of buying herself a flat and staying on in the town, but at the time she'd recently started a job in the local library and there were just too many people coming in who knew her, who had been friends or patients of her father's or who knew her from school. She was just too vulnerable, too open to pity, sympathy and well-meaning advice, to stay on there.

So she had followed in the footsteps of a million other hopeful young girls and gone to London to work in an office. And there she had met and fallen in love with Mark Kelsey. He was twenty-eight, good-looking, already a junior executive with an extremely promising future, and he had a wonderfully easy charm. How could she help but fall head over heels in love with him? For a year Alexa had known glorious happiness; happiness that had become perfect when Mark eventually asked her to marry him and they got engaged. Naturally she had wanted to be married at the old church in Seabrook where she had been christened and confirmed and her parents had been married before her, so Alexa had written to her oldest and closest friend, Elaine, who invited them to come and stay at her parents' home while they made all the arrangements. In her letter Elaine had said how much she was looking forward to meeting Mark and to being a bridesmaid. Only she hadn't been the bridesmaid— she had turned out to be the bride!

The worst moment of the day had come. Alexa got out of the car with the others and joined the knot of guests waiting to file down the receiving line. Elaine's parents were first, people she had known all her life and who had always been kind to her. Their faces became anxious, but somehow Alexa was able to smile at them and shake hands.

Elaine's mother gripped her hand tightly. 'Thank you for coming, my dear. I know how hard it must . . . how you must . . .' she broke off, biting her lip, and Alexa quickly took her hand away and moved on.

Mark's parents, too, she had liked very much. His father didn't say anything, just looked at her with a mixture of sympathy and admiration and gave her hand an encouraging squeeze. His mother, plainly embarrassed, said something, but Alexa didn't hear it, she was too aware that next she would have to greet the bride and groom. From somewhere she found the courage and strength to turn towards Mark with a cool smile on her lips.

Alexa didn't know it, but at that moment she looked very lovely. The coolness gave her poise and sophistication and the deliberate detachment in her manner added a touch of mystery. She quickly put out her hand so that there wouldn't be any mis-understanding about whether or not he should kiss her. She didn't think she could withstand the touch of his lips, even an impersonal peck on the cheek would be more than she could bear. Slowly he reached out and took her hand in his. Alexa forced herself to look into his face and their eyes met and held. Was he thinking the same thing that she was? Alexa wondered wildly. That it was she who should have been standing at his side in the white lace dress and not Elaine? But the only emotion that showed in his face was compassion.

Damn him! That was the last thing she needed. Fierce anger filled her, enabling her to say with ironic bitchiness, 'Congratulations. I always knew you'd make a dashing bridegroom.'

He started to say, 'Sandra, I . . .' but she quickly withdrew her hand and moved on to the bride.

'Elaine darling!' She kissed the air somewhere near the other girl's cheek, then stood back and ran her eyes over her. 'How *pretty* you look! I do *hope* you'll be happy.'

Turning away, she put the gift she was carrying into the hands of a waiting bridesmaid, and became aware of the best man, a larger and slightly older version of Mark, standing nearby, but she walked quickly over to where a waiter stood with a tray of drinks, took one, and drank it down almost in a gulp, without even tasting it. The crowd of people engulfed her, she wandered through it, found another waiter and took another drink, this time sipping it more slowly and discovering that it was dry sherry. Finding a quiet corner, she sat down on a reproduction Louis the Fourteenth settee and gave a sigh of relief. Now there was only the buffet to get through, together with the inevitable speeches and cutting the cake, before she could decently leave and catch a train back to London.

It would have been so much easier not to have come, for Mark and Elaine as well as herself, she supposed, but the whole town knew what had happened and a great many of them felt very sorry for her, especially coming so soon after the tragedy of losing her parents. So Elaine's mother had sent her a special invitation, with a letter asking her, for the sake of her lifelong friendship with Elaine, to attend.

Alexa smiled at a passing waiter, and in answer to the unspoken summons, he took her empty glass and gave her another full one.

She supposed she should have realised what was happening straightaway, but she hadn't. She had been so euphorically happy, taking Mark to Seabrook, showing him off to all her friends, that she hadn't noticed the way he looked at Elaine or the attention he showed her. Heaven help her, Alexa had just thought that he was being charming to her closest friend! Then had come his gradual withdrawal, the excuses for not taking her out in London, although he was always willing enough to go back to Seabrook to visit Elaine with her. Alexa, poor fool, had thought that being near her without being married was making him frustrated, and that he was only too eager to help finalise the wedding arrangements.

Then he told her. That he had fallen in love with Elaine the first time he had seen her, and that she felt the same way. That they had waited to tell her because they didn't want to hurt her. Alexa hadn't given in gracefully, she had put up a fight to try and keep him, but it hadn't done any good, nothing had been any good. She had lost him and she had to face it. Now there was only pride left. And bitterness. That, too, lay close under the surface veneer of detachment.

Alexa looked round the room of chattering, well-dressed people and knew suddenly that she would never come to Seabrook again. She had already left her job so that she didn't have to see Mark, and after today she would cut all ties with Elaine and her childhood. Perhaps, she thought drearily, I'll go abroad somewhere and settle there. But the thought held no appeal; nothing held any appeal any more.

Some old family friends came over to talk to her and she stayed with them until they moved into the room where the buffet was laid out on long, white damask-covered tables. There was wine to drink and she had several glasses, although she ate very little, and then of course there was champagne with the cake. The bride's father and then Mark made speeches and the best man read out the telegrams and made a speech too. He was so like Mark that she guessed he must be his elder brother who worked in America, and whose name she couldn't remember. It must have been a good speech, because everyone laughed and applauded, but Alexa took little notice, she kept looking at her watch and wondering when she could get away.

The speeches finished and she decided that she need only wait another ten minutes. A small group of musicians began to play quietly in the background and she sat and clutched her empty glass, waiting for the endless minutes to drag by.

'Let me fill that up again for you.'

He was so like his brother that for an instant Alexa thought it was Mark and gave a gasp of surprise, the colour flooding from her cheeks. Then, immediately, she realised who it was, but the mistake had unnerved her and she couldn't speak. Taking the glass from her hand, the best man filled it and gave it back to her, then filled the second glass he was carrying and set the bottle down on a small table nearby.

'I don't think we've met,' he remarked. 'I'm Mark's brother, Scott Kelsey.'

'How do you do,' she replied stiltedly.

'And you must be a friend or relation of the bride?' he prompted when she didn't go on.

Obviously he had no idea who she was. Slowly she said, 'I'm Alexandra Curtis,' and waited for embarrassment to show in his face and for him to apologise or to make an excuse and go away.

Neither happened. He merely nodded pleasantly and said, 'I work in South America and have only come back to England for the wedding, so I'm afraid I haven't had much time to get to know Elaine and her family. Are you a relation?'

'No, a friend. We used to go to school together when I lived in Seabrook.'

'You don't live here now?'

She shook her head. 'No. In London.'

She took a long drink of champagne and expected him to move on, but he showed no inclination to do so, instead asking her what she did.

Alexa shrugged. 'Oh, just secretarial work, but I'm between jobs at the moment. Just doing temp work until I find something that suits me.'

He filled her glass up again and she felt impelled to ask him about South America. Scott started telling her about Brazil and some project on the Amazon, but she wasn't really listening. Her eyes went restlessly round the room, wondering how she could get away, but then she saw Mark, his arm round Elaine's waist as they circulated among the guests, heading in her direction. Hastily she turned her back on them and gave his brother her full attention.

Superficially he was very like Mark, but he was taller, well over six feet, and broader across the shoulders, and he was very tanned. His face, too, lacked some of the casual charm that she had loved so much in Mark's; Scott's features had a sterner, more arrogant air, as if he was used to giving orders and having them obeyed. Altogether he was a tougher, less attractive version of his younger brother.

Out of the corner of her eye she saw that Mark and Elaine had safely gone by her and were lost among a group of other guests. She would be able to slip away unobserved.

'Alexandra is rather a mouthful,' Scott was saying. 'What do they usually call you—Alex?'

'No, Alexa.' Except Mark; he'd always used the other diminutive of her name—Sandra. But he was the only one, and she never wanted anyone else to call her that again. 'Look,' she went on hurriedly, 'it's nice to have met you, but I'm leaving now.'

His left eyebrow quirked in surprise. 'Already?'

'I have to catch a train back to London. And besides,' she improvised, 'big weddings like this aren't my scene.'

'Nor mine,' he said with a smile. 'But I've yet to meet a woman who didn't enjoy them.'

'Well, you just have,' Alexa said firmly, which was true enough; she was hating every minute of this one.

'You say you're going back to London?' Alexa nodded impatiently and he went on, 'I'm going there myself. And I have a car outside. Why don't we drive back together?'

'Oh, but I . . .'

She started to refuse, but he cut in, 'Just give me ten minutes to change out of this rig.' He gestured to his morning suit and gave her a crooked grin that was so like Mark's that her heart turned over. *So like Mark*. Alexa was too choked to speak and he took her silence for consent. 'Just ten minutes,' he repeated. 'See you in the lobby.'

Scott walked quickly out of the room while Alexa

stared after him numbly. Finishing her drink, she headed for the ladies' cloakroom, looking at herself in the glass and applying more lipstick with a shaky hand. She tried to think straight, but her mind felt fuddled and apathetic. Oh, God, she'd drunk too much champagne. Suppose she just walked out and forgot about him? But he might look for her and come after her to the station; you had to walk quite a long way down the High Street to reach it and he could easily overtake her in a car. She dithered over making a decision so long that she left it too late, he was already standing in the lobby when she came out of the cloakroom, dressed now in an ordinary suit and with a holdall at his feet. He was leaning on the reception desk writing a note, which he quickly folded and put into an envelope when he saw her. 'See that this gets to Mr Kelsey, senior, will you?' he said, handing it to the man behind the desk. Then he turned to her. 'All set?'

She nodded and he opened the main door for her and led her round the side of the hotel to the car park. He was using Mark's car, a silver Porsche that she had travelled in many times before. For a moment she drew back but he mistook her hesitation.

'Don't worry,' Scott assured her. 'I'm quite a safe driver.'

He opened the door for her, then dropped his bag in the back and got in beside her.

'Is this your car?' Alexa asked him in feigned innocence as he pulled away.

'No, it's Mark's. But he won't be needing it while he's on honeymoon so he's lent it to me until I go back.'

'Oh. Where are they going for the—the honeymoon?' she asked, finding it difficult to get the word out.

'To Hawaii.' Scott glanced at her in surprise. 'Didn't Elaine tell you?'

'Oh, yes. I forgot.'

She fell silent for a few moments as he negotiated the traffic in the busy High Street, and then remarked, 'Won't your parents think it rather odd of you leaving so early?'

He laughed and again her heart lurched in remembrance. 'They're probably not even surprised. They all know full well that I intensely disliked dressing up in that morning suit. I only did it to please Mark. He wanted everything to be perfect for Elaine. It seemed there'd been some unpleasantness at the beginning of their relationship because he was engaged to someone else who wouldn't let go, and he wanted to make it up to Elaine for that.' He looked across to where she sat gazing stonily ahead. 'I'm sorry, I suppose you know the other girl. Is she a friend?'

Slowly Alexa answered, 'I know her, yes. I've known her as long as I've known Elaine.' Abruptly she added, 'Did you mention me in that note you wrote for your father?'

Scott looked amused. 'No, I merely said that I was giving someone a lift and would phone them from London tomorrow.'

But they'd guess, Alexa thought. When they discovered that both of them were gone, Mark would guess. She turned her head to look at Scott and tried to see only the similarities to Mark. She remembered how much like his brother he had looked and sounded when he laughed and she deliberately set out to amuse him.

Alcohol always had the effect of bringing out her rather dry sense of humour, and that, together with her natural wit and a few droll remarks, soon had Scott laughing. He, too, had a sharp wit that could quickly pick up an idea and enlarge on it and his repartee, if anything, was more subtle and skilful than Mark's. Not that Alexa was any longer comparing the two, she was simply putting Scott in the void that Mark had left behind.

They stopped for dinner at a restaurant on the outskirts of London. Alexa went into the cloakroom and took off the loose jacket that matched the pink silk dress she was wearing. She was very slim, too thin really; she'd lost a lot of weight since Mark. Almost angrily she pushed that thought aside and took off her hat. She was wearing her hair up and, on impulse, she took one of the pink artificial flowers from her hat and fastened it in the side of her dark hair. More make-up followed and then she sprayed on some Miss Dior before standing back to look at herself. There, with the extra colour on her face and the jaunty flower in her hair, no one would ever think that this was the worst day of her life. Especially not Scott, not now that she'd deliberately set out to captivate him.

When she joined him, he looked her over in open appreciation and she tossed back her head and smiled in return. He put his arm round her waist as they walked towards the dining room; Alexa had a mental picture of Mark doing the same with Elaine at the wedding and she moved closer to Scott's side, felt his arm tighten and was fiercely glad.

They took their time over the meal, drinking gin and tonics while they studied the menu. Alexa was very gay, and Scott was obviously enjoying himself, laughing at the anecdotes she told him, quite oblivious to the fact that it was all a big act put on for his benefit. The food was deliciously cooked and presented, but Alexa hardly tasted it, although she had more than her share of the wine that went with it. She had the strangest feeling of being two people, one a puppet commanded by the other to be scintillatingly amusing, to sparkle and charm the big man sitting across the table, and all the while watching her own performance with detached interest.

There was a pocket-handkerchief dance floor in the restaurant and, after they had finished eating, Scott asked her to dance. The band was playing a slow number, fortunately one that didn't bring back any memories, and Alexa stood up willingly enough and let him take her in his arms. They moved slowly round the floor under the subdued lighting, her hand on his shoulder, but presently Scott drew her closer so that their bodies were touching, and she moved her hand up to run her fingers through the silky hairs at the back of his neck. She felt him draw in his breath, then he carried her other hand closer to his chest, bent his head and gently kissed her fingers. His dark eyes glittered down into hers. Alexa gave him a sensuous smile and rested her head against his shoulder as they danced.

Back at the table Scott ordered liqueurs: brandy for him and Benedictine for Alexa. She asked him about his childhood with Mark, a stab of almost welcome pain piercing her every time he mentioned his brother's name. It was as if the new pain cancelled out the old and left her numb. Scott reached out and took her hand as he talked, idly playing with her fingers. Suddenly he stopped talking, his hand gripping hers.

'Let's dance again,' he said thickly.

This time, by common consent, he held her very close, their hips moving against each other as they danced, both of them unaware of anyone else in the room. But halfway through the number Scott moved abruptly away from her. 'I think maybe we'd better leave,' he said raggedly, and firmly led her off the floor.

'All right. I'll get my things.'

In the car Alexa became animated again, teasing him a little so that his laugh rang out, rich and masculine—and so like Mark's. If she closed her eyes she could imagine that it was Mark sitting beside her. Scott drove more quickly now, picking his way through the suburban streets, handling the car skilfully and well. Alexa's flat was in St John's Wood and she had to direct him round the maze of one way streets.

'They've changed everything around since I was here last,' Scott remarked.

'When was that?'

'Over two years ago.'

So he must have gone to work in Brazil at about the same time as she'd started dating Mark, which was why she had never met him. How lucky. How very lucky.

'You take the next left,' she told him. 'And that's the entrance to my block, over there.'

He drew into a parking space and switched off the engine, turned to look at her.

'Are you staying at a hotel while you're in London?' she asked him.

'No, in Mark's flat.'

'Oh. Yes, of course.'

'Alexa?' He reached out and cupped her chin, ran his thumb gently along the line of her jaw. 'I want to see you again.'

'Do you?'

'Very much.' Leaning forward, he moved his hand

to the back of her neck, pulled her gently towards him and bent to kiss her. His lips were hard and firm against the full softness of hers, they explored her mouth, tasting, drinking in its richness. His kiss deepened, became more demanding, and Alexa slowly opened her mouth and responded to him. She felt his body quiver with passion and immediately drew away.

'I must go,' she said softly.

Scott's hand was still on her neck. Unsteadily he said, 'Do you live here alone?'

'Yes.'

'Then maybe I'd better walk you to your door?'

'All right. Thank you.'

They got out of the car and he locked it behind them before putting a hand under her elbow and walking her to the entrance. She had a key to the main door and another for her flat on the second floor. They climbed the stairs and at the door she turned to look at him.

'Perhaps you'd like to come in for a nightcap?'

'Thank you. I'd like that very much.'

Alexa turned to open the door, hiding her secret smile at the sudden gleam that had come into his eyes at her invitation. She turned on a lamp and moved over to the window to close the curtains, then gestured to the shelf unit. 'You'll find the drinks over there. Please help yourself—and I'll have a gin and tonic.'

A crazy kind of excitement filled her and Alexa had to go over to the rack and pretend to select a record to give herself time to try and control it. She found a smoochy L.P. and put it on the turntable, moved the arm across and let the stereos carry the soft melody into the room. When she turned back to Scott, she smiled, a puppet doll again.

He gave her her drink. 'Cheers!'

'Cheers.' It wasn't very strong, she finished hers almost in one go. Putting down the glass, she held out her hand and said huskily, 'We didn't finish that dance at the restaurant.'

'So we didn't.' He took her in his arms and they moved slowly in time to the music in the dim light thrown by the lamp, but that only lasted a few minutes before he bent his head to kiss her neck, working slowly, sensuously upwards to her ear, then along her jawline until he found her mouth. 'Alexa,' he breathed. 'Darling, I . . .'

But she put her arms round his neck, moving close to him, and kissed him ardently. He gave a kind of groan deep in his throat, kissing her back with a fierce hunger as passion took over. He slid a hand low down on her waist, holding her very close against him. Slowly, deliberately, she gyrated her hips until, with a fierce triumph, she felt his body harden with desire.

Lifting his head, Scott gripped her shoulders and stared down at her, his eyes dark with need. 'Alexa. Are you sure this is what you want?'

'Oh, yes, I'm sure. Very sure.' Standing on tiptoe to reach him, she gently began to kiss his lower lip with tiny, wanton little kisses.

He gave a gasp and his hands tightened, but he said, 'One way and another you've had quite a lot to drink today. I wouldn't want you to regret this . . .'

Alexa silenced him by deliberately putting her mouth over his, searching and demanding to be kissed. After a while she moved away and smiled at him. 'But I'm at my best after I've had a few drinks,' she told him seductively.

For a moment surprise showed in his eyes, but then he smiled knowingly in return and allowed her to take him by the hand and lead him into the bedroom. Alexa would have left the room in darkness, but he flipped on the light and shut the door behind them. She turned and waited for him.

Scott slipped off his jacket and dropped it on a chair before coming over to her. He didn't kiss her as she expected him to, instead reaching up to take the flower out of her hair and then the pins, so that it fell in a tumbling dark cloud around her shoulders.

'I've been wanting to do that since the first moment I met you,' he said softly. Lifting his left hand, he entwined it in her hair, enjoying the soft silkiness, letting it run through his palm and over his fingers.

Alexa stood still, her eyes closed, letting him do what he wanted. She felt him gently running his finger across the fine, dark arch of her eyebrows and heard his voice, Mark's voice, say huskily, 'Oh, Alexa, you're so lovely. So very lovely.' His finger ran slowly on down the outline of her small, straight nose and on across her lips, pausing to take in the sensual fullness of the lower one that trembled under his touch, then on down the firm roundness of her chin.

'Open your eyes,' he commanded.

Slowly, reluctantly, she obeyed.

'You have such beautiful eyes,' he murmured. 'I've never seen any of quite that colour blue before. Like the deep blue of periwinkles or a Mediterranean sky in summer.'

Alexa stared at him for a long moment, then said abruptly, 'Put out the light! Please put out the light.'

Surprise again showed in his face, but then he said, 'All right, if that's what you want,' and crossed to turn it off.

Blessed darkness filled the room and now she didn't have to close her eyes to pretend, to lose herself in the world where she most wanted to be. He came back to her and she reached up to take off his tie and then slowly undo the buttons of his shirt—Mark's shirt. His chest was as smooth as she remembered from the days when they had gone bathing together. Dreamily she ran her fingers over him, exploring, teasing, then undoing the cuffs and letting the shirt fall to the floor to lie in the little bar of light that came under the door. His hands went to the zip of her dress, pulling it slowly down. The straps slipped off her shoulders and then somehow it was on the floor around her feet. Alexa kicked it aside impatiently, and returned his hot, hungry kisses as he unhooked her bra strap and his hands caressed her breasts.

For the first time she moaned, lost now in her fantasy dream, feeling Mark's hands on her body, hearing his voice as he told her how beautiful she was, how much he wanted her. He began to take off the rest of her clothes, his hands knowledgeable and experienced, but taking time to explore and fondle. Tremors of desire ran through her when he drew her slowly against him and she felt his bare flesh against her own. His skin was like silk, but hot, so hot. Alexa moved her breasts against his chest, making him groan as he felt her breasts harden.

Scooping back the bedclothes, he picked her up and laid her gently on the bed, then she heard him take off the rest of his clothes. He didn't get into bed with her straightaway, instead sitting on the edge letting his eyes devour the slim youthfulness of her white body outlined in the semi-darkness: the curves of her firm uptilted breasts, slender waist, and the length of her shadowed hips and long, shapely legs. Gently he stroked the dark hair spread across the whiteness of the pillow and murmured, 'Darling, your body is perfect. Exquisite.'

Alexa smiled, her eyes still closed. It was what she had expected Mark to say tonight—their wedding night. Lifting her arms out to him, she said softly, 'Hold me. Hold me close.'

He slid on to the bed beside her and she gave a little cry of wonder as she felt his nakedness along the whole length of her body. His skin was so firm, and yet so soft. He began to kiss her eyes, her neck, her mouth, and on down to her breasts. Desire rose in her like a storm and she held his head there, her fingers coiled in his hair, wanting him to go on and on. But presently his hands moved down, making her gasp and arch her body towards him, on fire with need.

'Oh, God, Alexa. You're the most exciting woman I've ever met!' His mouth was on hers again, hot and feverish, his breath ragged and uneven. She could hear his heart hammering in his chest. He moved on top of her and she gasped as she felt his heavy masculinity pinning her down, his strength dominating her. Their bodies were burning hot and slippery with perspiration. Alexa dug her nails into his shoulders, but he didn't even feel it.

Their legs twined and she arched her hips against him, her body speaking its need, wanting him to fill the great emptiness inside her. She moaned again, her mouth against his shoulder, biting into his flesh. Oh, dear God, it was so wonderful! But she had always known that it would be like this, that she and Mark would make wonderful, ecstatic love together.

'Alexa.' Hoarsely he said her name. 'I want you. I want you, darling.'

She felt him lift himself up on his elbows and for a moment tried to restrain him, to keep him close, but then he parted her legs with insistent urgency and she

knew that the moment she had longed for had come at
last.

'Oh, yes. Yes!' Exultation filled her and she cried
out with happiness. 'Oh, Mark, Mark. I love you so
much! Take me, darling. Oh, Mark, please love me!'

CHAPTER TWO

SCOTT'S body stiffened, grew rigid, but Alexa was so lost in her own ecstasy and anticipation that she didn't even know anything was wrong until he reached out an arm, knocking things over on the bedside cabinet as he sought the lamp and switched it on.

The light brought her back to reality with a sickening lurch. She saw Scott's face staring down at her and immediately closed her eyes again. 'Turn it off. Turn it off!' she ordered, her voice rising on a shrill, desperate note.

'Oh, no!' He slid off her and pulled her head back towards him when she tried to turn away. 'I want to know just who you think I am.'

Alexa smiled and ran her hands down his chest, trying to placate him, desperate to get back where they were a few second ago. 'Did I get your name wrong? I'm sorry—it must have been the drink. I didn't mean it, really. I don't even know him.' She parted her lips into a sexy pout and moved her legs against his. 'Does it matter, darling? When we both want each other so much.'

For a moment longer he hesitated, but she began to run her lips down his neck and across his chest, sucking, biting, and she felt him relax and his hands start to move over her again.

After a few minutes she whispered, 'Turn off the light.'

'No, I want to look at you,' he muttered, his voice thick again.

Alexa closed her eyes tightly, trying to lose herself once more, but it wasn't the same. Angrily she said, 'Damn you, turn if off! I like it better in the dark.'

Scott gave a dry chuckle and bit the lobe of her ear.' 'Little spitfire!' But he moved to obey her.

He seemed to take a long time. Alexa murmured urgently, breathlessly, 'Hurry! I want you so much, I want you to love me.'

His voice, when he spoke, sounded strange. 'You said that you don't know Mark?'

'No.' She hastened to reassure him. 'I never met him until today.'

His voice, cold as ice, said, 'Then just how do you explain having a photograph of the two of you on your bedside table?'

Slowly Alexa opened her eyes, knowing that she'd lost the beautiful dream, that all chance of it was gone for ever. Rolling away from him, she sat on the edge of the bed with her back to him, grabbing up her towelling robe from the foot rail. 'Get out of here!' she shouted furiously as she dragged it on.

'You've got some explaining to do first.'

'I have nothing to say to you. Just get out of my home!'

She got up, fastening the robe around her, and headed for the bathroom, but Scott came after her and caught her wrist. 'Oh, no, you don't. I want to know exactly what kind of game you're playing!' He dragged her back and pushed her when her legs came up against the bed so that she fell down on it again. 'Now, who are you?' he demanded.

Alexa's head swam and she felt dizzy. She lifted her head to glare at him and saw him towering over her, his body heavily tanned and still naked. Hastily she turned away. 'Can't you, for God's sake, put some clothes on?'

He moved away and Alexa lay back on the pillow, feeling sick inside, realising what she'd done through the drunken haziness in her mind and hating herself with fierce disgust.

Scott came to sit on the edge of the bed and shook her none too gently. 'Don't go to sleep. You've got some talking to do.'

Reluctantly she opened her eyes and saw that he was almost fully dressed, his shirt just open at the neck. He picked up the photograph and looked at it more closely, reading the inscription. It said simply 'To Sandra, my love always, Mark'.

Scott frowned. 'Sandra? But surely that was the name of the girl Mark used to be engaged to.' Enlightenment dawned and his eyes widened. 'But of course, it's another way of shortening Alexandra! So *you're* his ex-fiancée?'

For a brief instant anger filled her, she felt like shouting out: I'm the girl he was in love with, he should have married me! Me, not Elaine. He jilted me. Can't you understand? He jilted me! But all she could say in a small, lost voice, was 'Yes.'

He stared down at her, working it all out, and she could guess that he had arrived at the right answer when she saw the flare of anger in his face. 'And you couldn't have Mark, so you decided to use me as a substitute.' His lip curled in distaste. 'My God, you're something else!' Angrily he caught hold of her arm and made her sit up. 'And that's why you wanted the light off, wasn't it? Wasn't it?' he shouted furiously when she didn't answer. 'So that you could pretend you were with him?'

'Yes! All right. Yes!' Alexa put her hands up over her face, her body trembling. But not with fear, only in deeper self-hatred as it was brought out into the open.

Scott stood up and she thought with relief that he was going to leave, but instead he began to stride angrily up and down in the small confines of the bedroom, dwarfing it. Then he swung round on her. 'And just what was the idea of going to the wedding? To spoil it for them? To be the skeleton at their marriage feast?' he demanded savagely.

'They invited me,' Alexa answered dully.

'And of course you had to go. Didn't it occur to you that your being there would spoil their happiness?'

Alexa didn't bother to try to explain. Depression settled on her like a thick black cloud. She wanted him to go so that she could be alone with this jagged misery that was far worse than all the pain and heartache that had gone before. But, if anything, his anger had increased.

'And just how the hell was I supposed to feel in all this?' Scott demanded forcefully. 'Do you think I enjoy being used? I suppose you'd have thrown me out the minute you woke up in the morning and found that it wasn't Mark in bed beside you?' He glared down at her balefully. 'I ought to put on every light in the place and force you to keep your eyes open while I take you. Maybe then you'd realise just which man you were having sex with,' he threatened, adding with abhorrence, 'My God, you make me sick!'

Alexa shuddered at his words, knowing that she deserved them all and unable in her state of utter wretchedness and self-condemnation to realise that his anger resulted as much from hurt pride as disgust. Slowly she dragged herself off the bed and stood up. 'Please go away,' she said in a dull, flat tone that was little more than a whisper.

'Why, so that you can switch off the lights and start fantasising again?'

Alexa flinched as if he'd struck her. 'Just leave me alone!' she cried out in sudden despair. 'Do you hear me? Just go away and leave me alone!' Lifting her hands, she buried her head in them, her body swaying in pain and misery.

Scott hesitated a moment, then moved to her and tried to pull her arms down. 'Alexa, listen to me . . .'

But she pulled away from him and shouted hysterically, 'Get away from me! Just go away!'

'You're in no state to be left on your own. You'd better let me . . .'

As he spoke he took hold of her, but Alexa tore free with sudden strength, flinging her arm upwards and catching him across the face as she did so.

'Why, you little bitch!' He lunged for her again, but she fought him off in a kind of fierce, maddened panic and ran into the bathroom, slamming the door and bolting it behind her before he could stop her.

'Alexa, open this door!' He rattled the handle angrily, but she took no notice.

For a few moments after pulling on the light she looked hazily round the windowless room, wondering what she was doing there and seeing it only as a place of refuge. Scott began to hammer on the door and she put her hands up over her ears to shut out the noise. She felt very tired, deathly tired, and her reflection in the mirror was pale as a ghost with just her eyes two dark patches staring back at her.

It came to her quite suddenly what she had to do. Without any hesitation or second thoughts she opened the bathroom cabinet and scrabbled around inside to find the almost full bottle of aspirins. There was a glass on the shelf and she automatically began to rinse it under the tap until she realised suddenly that it didn't matter. That brought her up short for a minute and she heard Scott's voice on a sharp, suspicious note call, 'Alexa? What are you doing? Open the door!'

Hastily she filled the glass and emptied a handful of tablets into her palm. She began to cram them into her mouth, some of them falling into the basin and water spilling down her chin as she tried to swallow them down. Inevitably some got stuck in her throat and she began to choke and cough.

'Alexa, for God's sake open the door!'

But she went on swallowing the pills, concentrating on what she was doing, oblivious to the sounds of something smashing against the door. Tears began to run down her face, but she didn't know why she was crying until she realised that she would never see Mark again. She said his name on an agonised note of longing and then put more aspirins into her mouth.

The door suddenly burst open, the bolt ripped from its screws, and Scott stood framed in the doorway. He took in the situation at a glance, had been expecting it, and sprang towards her, knocking the aspirins out of her hand. Alexa turned on him in a fury and tried to fight him, clawing at his face, but she was no match for his masculine strength.

'Let me die,' she begged him, weeping hysterically. 'Please leave me alone. Can't you see I don't want to live any more?'

'You bitch!' Scott swore at her. 'You bloody stupid little bitch!'

There followed five very nasty minutes as he dragged her bodily over to the loo and thrust his fingers down her throat to make her sick. Alexa gasped and retched, pleading with him to let her go, but he took hold of her by the hair, forcing her head down until she just couldn't be sick any more. Then he pulled her to her feet and made her walk up and down, up and down so that she wouldn't go to sleep. It seemed to go on and on endlessly, Scott holding her up and forcing her to stagger along while she clung to him, begging him to leave her alone.

At some point he left her in the armchair for a few minutes and she immediately fell asleep, but he was soon back with black coffee, so hot that it scalded her mouth when he forced her to drink it. The night seemed to go on for ever, Scott slapping her face or shaking her whenever she tried to go to sleep. But, at last, when the first faint light of dawn crept through the curtains, he picked her up and carried her into the bedroom, laid her on the bed and pulled the duvet over her. Immediately Alexa's eyes began to close and a great feeling of thankfulness filled her. 'Mark,' she murmured. 'Mark, darling,' as she fell into a deep, deep sleep.

Waking was like making a very long journey that was a great uphill struggle. Like taking one step forward and sliding two steps back. Her eyes would open a little and she would try to stay awake, but then they felt so heavy that she just had to close them, only to open them a while later and try to fight her way through the thick, cotton-woolly cloud that seemed to be inside her brain. She moved on the pillow and groaned as a stab of pain shot through her head. And her throat felt so dry and furry, horrible! She tried to think why she felt like this, but her head ached too much to concentrate. She groaned again and a voice said roughly, 'Here, sit up and drink this. It will make you feel better.'

Her eyes came wide open at that, but she had to blink because the room was filled with sunlight, but not the bright clear light of morning, this was the rich, deep pink glow of sunset that streamed through the window. Slowly, uncomprehendingly, she obediently sat up and stared at the man bending over her. She took the glass of water that he held out, and only then did it all come flooding back.

'Oh, God!' Her hands began to tremble violently and some of the liquid spilled from the glass. Scott's strong hand came down to cover hers, holding it steady.

'Drink it,' he commanded again.

The water was very cool and refreshing. Alexa thought that she'd never tasted anything quite so wonderful as it healed her parched throat. When she had done Scott took the glass and looked down at her grimly. Alexa took one glance at his face and quickly lowered her head. But then she became aware that her robe had come open while she slept, revealing her breasts, and she hastily covered herself, pulling the material together with nervous fingers.

'What's—what's the time?' she mumbled.

'Almost eight. You slept the clock round.'

Alexa sneaked another glance at Scott and saw that his mouth was set into a thin line, his face hard and implacable. She remembered the way she had lured him into her bed the previous night and grew hot with embarrassment. No wonder he'd been angry; he'd had every right.

He must have noticed her embarrassment, but he merely said, 'How are you feeling?'

'All right, I suppose. My head aches.'

'Perhaps you'd like a couple of aspirins?'

The acid sarcasm in his voice made Alexa lift her head and look into his cold grey eyes. The condemnation she read there made her flush even deeper and bite her lip. He hadn't wasted any time in bringing it out into the open. And now she had to try and face up to what she had done—or tried to do.

That she hadn't succeeded was due entirely to this big stranger who was regarding her with such distaste. The whole thing was such a sordid mess that for a moment Alexa tried to push it out of her mind, to pretend that it had never happened, but Scott Kelsey was still standing there looming over her like a black cloud of conscience.

Slowly, stumblingly, she said, 'I want to apologise for last night. I'm sorry that you—that you got involved.'

Scott hooked forward a chair and sat down beside the bed, his position relaxed and casual but his eyes watching her like a hawk. 'Let's get it quite clear just what you're apologising for, shall we? Is it for trying to use me as a substitute for Mark, or for attempting suicide?' he demanded. Adding sarcastically, 'Or maybe you're saying that you're sorry I got involved and stopped you from taking the easy way out?'

Alexa flinched and looked away. He seemed to expect some kind of an answer, but she had no strength to argue his accusations. Her head ached with a sharp, piercing pain that made her want to keep her eyes tight closed, and her brain felt terribly heavy and clogged. At length she said into the silence, 'Thank you for staying with me, but I'm fine now. You mustn't let me keep you any longer.'

The phrase sounded stupidly formal and out of place in the circumstances, like a hostess politely trying to get rid of a guest who was beginning to overstay his welcome. But really that was just what it was; she wanted so much to be left alone and not have him sitting looking at her like that. How could she even begin to probe her own feelings and emotions when Scott made it so plain exactly what he thought of her.

'Oh, I'm in no hurry,' he told her over-casually. 'I guess I'll stay around for a while.'

'Look,' she pursued rather desperately, 'you needn't think I'll do anything—anything silly. I won't, I promise you. It was just that I was—that I'd had rather too much to drink yesterday, that's all. I won't do it again.'

'Won't you?' he replied sceptically. 'What guarantee have I got of that?'

'I—I've promised I won't,' she answered, groping for some means of proving to him that she meant it, but unable to find more convincing words.

Scott got to his feet suddenly, standing over her like some dark bird of prey. 'You miserable little liar! Do you really think I'm fool enough to believe that? As soon as I'm out of the way you'll behave just like the coward you are and try and get rid of yourself again!'

'No, I won't,' Alexa said urgently. 'I've told you, I . . .'

'You've told me just a bit too often,' Scott interrupted harshly. 'People who protest too much usually intend to do just the opposite.'

Alexa leant back on the headboard and stared at him, quite unable to get through to him. A wave of black depression hit her and she said sharply, 'Well, you can't stay with me for ever, can you?'

His eyes narrowed. 'No, I can't,' he agreed slowly. 'But maybe I can keep you with me until you get enough guts to face the fact that Mark preferred Elaine to you.'

The choice of words had been meant to hurt. Alexa's face paled and she pulled the duvet closer around her, burying her tightly-clenched fingers in its softness. It took a moment for the rest of his words to sink in. 'What do you mean, keep me with you?' a twinge of pain in her head making her frown and close her eyes again.

Steadily Scott answered, 'I've decided to take you back to Brazil with me.'

Her eyes flew open and she stared at him stupidly. 'What did you say?'

'You heard me. I'm going to take you with me to Brazil.'

'But—but you can't!' Alexa gaped at him, her brain refusing to take it in.

'Oh, yes, I can. Who's to stop me?'

'I will. I won't go with you. You can't make me,' she retorted, glaring at him defiantly.

He didn't raise his voice, didn't even sound very threatening, but there was distinct menace in his tone as he said softly, 'Oh, yes, I can.'

Alexa's tiny flame of defiance died stillborn. Somehow she knew that he meant what he said and that he would be quite capable of carrying out his threat. She shook her head from side to side in dazed puzzlement. 'But why?' she asked despairingly. 'What does it matter to you whether I live or die? Why should you care what happens to me?'

'I don't,' he replied with brutal candour. 'As far as I'm concerned you can go to hell as soon as, and by whatever method, you choose.'

'Then—then why?' she faltered, her face paler now at his lack of feeling.

'For Mark's sake, of course. Don't tell me that you haven't already realised what your suicide would do to his marriage. It would be ruined from the outset. Mark and Elaine would have your death on their consciences for the rest of their lives, continually coming between them. No marriage, however strong, could withstand that.'

'Oh God,' Alexa said softly. 'I hadn't thought of that.'

'No?' Scott asked jeeringly. 'Do you really expect me to believe that?'

'I hadn't, I tell you.' Then, dully, 'But either way it doesn't matter; I've told you that I won't try it again and I meant it.' She looked up at him pleadingly. 'Truly, Scott. Please believe me. I was—upset by the wedding, that's all. I got depressed, and drinking helped. And then you—you looked so like Mark.' She found it hard to plead so abjectly, and it made little difference anyway.

Looking at her sardonically, Scott said, 'Maybe right now you really believe that you won't do it again, but what's to stop you, the next time you get depressed, taking a few drinks to try and get over it and then trying to commit suicide when you've had enough alcohol?' He shook his head. 'No, Alexa, I'm not prepared to take the risk.'

Alexa looked at him unhappily, noting the obstinately determined thrust of his jaw and realising that now just wasn't the right time to start arguing with him. Pulling the robe tightly around her, she got out of bed and stood up. 'I'm going to have a bath,' she stated flatly.

Scott came round to her side and took her arm firmly. 'No baths. But you can take a shower.'

She looked at him indignantly, then saw the reasoning behind his order; you couldn't drown yourself in a shower. For an instant she felt physically sick, but whether with him or with herself she wasn't sure. Turning abruptly away, she padded on bare feet into the bathroom. The bolt had broken completely off the door and was gone, along with what was left of the bottle of aspirins. Scott left her to have her shower and, when Alexa looked in the cabinet, she found that several other items were gone too. He had removed all the few boxes and bottles of patent medicines that she had kept there, as well as one or two other items like her nail file and scissors. What the hell did he think she was going to do—slash her wrists? That that was exactly what he thought brought Alexa up short. She stood under the shower, letting the water run over her, and for the first time the full enormity of what she had tried to do hit her. Tears ran down her cheeks, and her only comfort was that Scott couldn't see or hear her cry.

After ten minutes he banged on the door. 'Okay, you've had long enough. Come on out or I'll come and get you!'

Alexa lifted her hand to the shower tap and then grew still, wondering whether she dared defy him, but she had no strength of either body or mind to fight the conviction in his voice and her hand carried on and obediently turned off the tap. She towelled herself dry and put the robe on again while she went into the bedroom to get herself some clothes. Scott had gone into the sitting-room, she could see him through the partly open door, sitting at his ease in the armchair, smoking a cigarette, his long legs stretched out in front of him. But, despite his apparent casualness, there was an animal quality about him, something coiled and watchful, ready to spring into life at any second. Alexa hesitated a moment, staring at his hard profile, her tired brain trying to work out how to handle the man and the situation, but then, as if he had felt her eyes on him, he turned his head to look at her.

Alexa flushed, as if she had been caught out at something, and angrily reached out to push the door shut. When she had dressed and brushed her hair, she felt a little better, but her head still ached, was heavy and woozy. Her body, too, felt as if all the strength had drained out of it. When she came out of the bedroom, she heard Scott moving about in the tiny kitchen, and the table in the sitting-room had been set ready for a meal. She noticed, too, a strange leather suitcase standing near the front door.

As she stood looking at it, Scott pushed open the kitchen door and came in carrying two plates of food.

'Is that your suitcase?' she asked him hesitantly.

'Yes.'

'When did you bring it here?'

'While you were asleep. It was down in the car.' She hesitated again before asking the next, obvious question, but Scott said briskly, 'Come and eat. We'll talk about it afterwards.'

He had made omelettes and a salad, with slices of wholemeal bread. Suddenly hungry, Alexa cleaned her plate and let him pour her out another cup of coffee. Only then did the incongruity of it all strike her; sitting here with this man who, in the measurement of time, was almost a total stranger, but as far as emotions went, with whom she had almost reached the very heights and the darkest depths.

They had eaten in silence, but as Alexa sipped her second cup of coffee, Scott broke it by saying quite matter-of-factly, 'I shall be staying here with you until we leave for Brazil.'

Alexa's hand shook, but she tried to stay calm as she answered, 'I've told you, I'm not coming with you. I don't want to go to Brazil.'

'No? Then where do you want to go to?'

She shrugged helplessly. 'I don't want to go anywhere. I just want to stay here.'

Scott's mouth twisted sneeringly. 'So that you can

drown in self-pity again? So that you can buy another bottle of aspirins to take the next time you drink yourself into a stupor of depression? My God, Alexa, what a spineless creature you are!'

'I won't,' she tried to protest, but it was like beating her head against a stone wall, and now there was the smallest note of doubt in her voice. He was so sure, so convinced that she would try it again that it rocked her own certainty that she wouldn't. Because never in her wildest dreams had Alexa imagined that she would do anything so unhinged, so completely lacking in control, as trying to end her life. She just wasn't the type. She had always thought herself too strong, too self-controlled for anything like that. Which just showed you how wrong you can be, how little you can know yourself or how you'll react in an emotional crisis.

'If I left you alone,' Scott was saying, 'what would you do? You don't have a steady job to take your mind off things, and you don't have any close relations to look after you.'

'How do you know that?'

Scott took out a packet of cigarettes and lit one. 'I did some phoning while you were asleep and made a few enquiries about you.'

Alexa's blue eyes opened wide. 'You phoned your parents? Did you—did you tell them about me? About—about . . .?'

'No.' His eyes narrowed as he blew out a small cloud of smoke. He seemed to be watching carefully for her reaction. 'Would it have mattered if I had?'

She nodded slowly, realising a little of just how much she would have cared, how ashamed she would have felt. Tiredness hit her again suddenly and she pushed the thought to one side, her emotions too lacerated to have the strength to cope with it.

'Do you have any really close friends?' Scott went on.

'No, I only had—Elaine.'

'No other friends?'

'Oh, yes. Lots of other *friends*. But only one that I'd been close to all my life, that I would have done anything for and trusted implicitly,' Alexa replied with harsh bitterness.

Scott looked at her for a long moment, then brought her back to his original question. 'So if I left you alone, what would you do?'

She shrugged helplessly. 'I don't know. Get a job, I suppose. I thought of going away somewhere.'

'Where?'

'I don't know.' Apathy settled over her like a thick, heavy blanket. 'I don't care.'

Grinding out his cigarette, Scott stood up. 'Good. In that case you can have no objection to coming to Brazil,' he said briskly. 'If you don't care where you go you might just as well give in gracefully and make up your mind to the fact that I'm taking you with me.'

'But I . . .'

'Stop arguing, Alexa. It's settled. It has been right from the start.' He looked down at her jeeringly. 'And you have nowhere else to go, remember? Except back into your own personal hell, of course.'

Gripping the edge of the table, she stared up at him nervously. 'But with you—I won't be free.'

His hard, handsome face grew contemptuous. 'You'll never be free, Alexa. Not until you learn to grow up and face whatever life deals out to you—even if it only kicks you in the teeth.'

They spent the night in the flat together: Alexa slept

in the bed while Scott made himself comfortable on the put-u-up settee in the sitting-room. She had fallen asleep almost immediately, but the residue of the aspirins eventually wore off and Alexa woke again just as the first light of morning filtered through the curtains. Her head still felt heavy, but the sharp ache had gone. At first she tried to go to sleep again, but it was impossible; her mind was too full and she stirred restlessly.

Her thoughts were a confused jumble, continuously going back over the horrible, inglorious mess she'd made of things after the wedding. And the future she could hardly bear to think about, because she just couldn't see one. Not among people who knew her, at any rate. For the first time she tried to rationally consider going to Brazil with Scott. After all, what alternative did she have to think about? And the idea did have its attractions. It would be somewhere completely new where no one knew her. Presumably Scott had a job in Rio de Janeiro or one of the other cities and a place to live, so she would have somewhere to stay. And if she didn't like it she could always leave. She had plenty of money for her fare, and even though Scott had spoken so grimly of keeping an eye on her, there was no way he could watch her twenty-four hours a day. He would have to go to work and she could leave then, when and if she wanted to. And in the meantime, if he was so insistent on taking her with him, then he could provide for her and take care of her. His reason for wanting to do so, Alexa pushed firmly out of her mind, afraid to even admit the possibility that he might be right.

Against all that, though, there were of course very definite disadvantages. The biggest, in more ways than one, was Scott's physical presence. He was such a strong personality, so sure of himself and what he wanted. Alexa wasn't quite sure whether she was afraid of him or not. She was certainly afraid of his sarcasm and writhed under his contempt, but she was also instinctively sure that he was quite capable of looking after her, and right now she desperately needed someone to lean on and make the decisions for her.

Impulsively she got out of bed and padded silently across the bedroom to the door, opening it as quietly as she could and moving across to the side of the settee. There was just enough light for her to make out his head turned towards her on the pillow. Even in repose his features didn't look relaxed, it was as if he was waiting for something to wake him and bring him immediately alert. The only signs of gentleness about his face were the rather long eyelashes that brushed his cheeks and the lock of thick dark hair that had fallen forward over his forehead. Did she really want to go to Brazil with this stranger—a stranger whom she only had to look at to be reminded of the man she loved, of what might have been? He had said that he would make her go, but he must know that there was no way he could do so against her will, not if she really didn't want to. Forcing her tired brain to work, Alexa supposed that really it boiled down to the question of whether she wanted to stay in London and inevitably hear from one source or another about Mark and Elaine or whether to get right away and try to forget. And if the latter, she might just as well go with Scott as try to make out somewhere new all by herself.

As she gazed down at him as if trying to find the answer in his face, Scott opened his eyes to look at her and she knew that he'd been awake all the time.

'Well?' he demanded. 'Seen enough?'

'Yes,' Alexa replied slowly, 'I have seen enough. I'll come with you to Brazil.'

He smiled thinly. 'Did you really think you had a choice?'

The following day he spent a lot of time on the phone, then made her sign a couple of forms which she couldn't be bothered to even read, and demanded her birth certificate to give to a special messenger who called at the flat for it, presumably for a visa or something, Alexa supposed. He made her call her landlord and tell him that she would be giving up the flat at the end of the week and to arrange for any furniture that she wanted to keep to be put in storage. There were a few antique pieces that she had brought from her parents' home that she didn't want to part with, but the rest was modern stuff that she'd bought when she moved in and, looking round at it, she realised that although she'd once been quite proud of the things, she now couldn't care less if they were sold.

Apathy began to set in again and she would have just sat around all day, but Scott kept her busy, packing her clothes, sorting out books for the local hospital, blankets for Oxfam. If he went out he made her go with him and he watched her like a hawk, his hand firmly under her elbow as he piloted her around. Physically she had recovered except for occasional tremors in her limbs that came whenever something brought back to her the enormity of what she had tried to do: when Scott firmly pulled her back from the kerb as a big red London double-decker bus was about to thunder by, or when she saw flowers growing in a park and realised that she might never have seen them again. It was probably only some kind of delayed shock, but it was enough to make her feel afraid and unsure of herself. Emotionally, too, she was glad to have Scott to lean on. She went round in an apathetic daze, meekly following his orders and letting him organise her and keep her busy, because that way she didn't have to think about Mark on honeymoon with Elaine, lying with her on the beach or in bed, holding her in his arms, making love to her.

Scott contacted a dealer who came to look at her furniture and carpets, agreed a price and arranged to clear the stuff after they had left. The storage people came to carefully crate up her antiques and wanted to know how long they were to be stored. Alexa frowned in perplexity; she hadn't given any thought to the distant future, her thoughts hadn't gone further than Friday when they left for Brazil, and even that seemed an eon of time away. She looked at Scott for guidance.

He hesitated for a moment, then said briefly, 'We'll be back in England in four months.'

Four months. Did he really expect her to have got over Mark by then? she wondered bitterly. Didn't he realise that she'd never get over him?

On Wednesday he took her out with him to order some supplies that he wanted to be sent out after him. They ordered most of the goods from Harrods and Alexa was bewildered by the amount of things he wanted; foodstuffs such as tinned fruit cake as well as cases of wine and a whole load of medicinal items.

'What on earth do you want all those for?' Alexa demanded in astonishment.

Scott gave her a quick glance; it was the first sign of interest she had shown since she had agreed to go with him. 'They're scarce in parts of Brazil. People are glad to get them.'

He waited for her to ask him why, but Alexa had already lost interest and stood silently waiting for him to finish.

When they got back to the flat there was a large envelope addressed to him on the doormat. It had been brought round by hand. Scott picked it up and slit it open, took out the papers inside. He read them through and then followed her to the bedroom where Alexa was brushing her hair. Leaning on the door jamb, he said deliberately, 'I've just received the special licence that will enable us to be married on Friday morning.'

For a moment Alexa thought she hadn't heard him correctly. Slowly she lowered the hairbrush and turned to stare at him. '*What* did you say?'

'You heard me,' he answered calmly. 'I said we're going to be married on Friday morning.'

'But I—but I don't want to marry you!'

He smiled grimly. 'You don't have any choice. They don't allow unmarried European women on the project where I work. Irregular relationships are frowned on.'

Alexa continued to stare at him, her mind in a riot. For a few minutes she still couldn't believe it, thought in her bewilderment that he must be playing a joke. But the set, determined look on his face soon disabused her of that; Scott Kelsey wasn't the kind of man who played jokes, especially about something like this. He was deadly serious. She realised that he must have meant this from the start and remembered that he had borrowed her birth certificate and the forms he had got her to sign.

'Why didn't you tell me before?' she demanded accusingly.

He looked at her narrowly and replied slowly, 'If you really want to know, it was because I was afraid you might panic and do something stupid again.'

A rush of colour filled her cheeks and Alexa got

hastily to her feet, tightly gripping the hairbrush and holding it like a weapon. 'I've told you time and again that I won't. Why can't you believe me?'

Scott didn't answer, just looked at her eloquently.

Alexa flushed again and said determinedly, 'I'm not going to marry you. I don't want to. And—and I'm quite sure *you* don't want to marry *me*.'

'You're right,' he agreed laconically. 'But I've already told you that they don't allow unmarried women on the site, so there's no help for it.'

'But—but there must be!' Alexa wailed.

'You don't have to worry, the marriage will be nothing more than a formality, just a legal piece of paper to enable us to go to Brazil. It can quite easily be annulled when we get back to England.' His grey eyes ran over her in cold disdain. 'You surely didn't think that I'd want to claim any rights, did you?'

That aspect hadn't even occurred to her; it was the thought of marrying any man other than Mark that had jolted her so violently out of her apathy, that and the natural reaction of anyone who has a totally unexpected and alien idea thrust at them. The night that they had first met, when she had taken him into her bed, Alexa had resolutely pushed out of her mind. And it had been possible to do so because Scott, too, had never referred to it again. In the ensuing days he had shown absolutely no interest in her as a woman at all, had made no attempt to even touch her except to take her arm in his firm grip whenever he felt it necessary. And she hadn't expected him to, had taken it for granted that he no longer wanted her.

Alexa looked at him now, standing so tall and arrantly masculine in the doorway. That he had a strong sexual appetite and experience with women he had proved beyond a shadow of doubt that night, so could she trust him to keep his word and stay at a distance while they were in Brazil? His face was still cold, still contemptuous, his mouth twisted into a cynically mocking smile as if he guessed her thoughts. Only then did Alexa start to have some idea of what effect the kind of treatment that she had dished out could have on a man. To be used sexually could only denigrate any man, but to be used as a sexual substitute for another man, and that his own brother . . . Alexa couldn't hope to understand the blow that it had been to his ego, but she *could* see how it had completely changed his behaviour towards her.

Now he treated her with open dislike, and she realised that he would probably go on doing so while they were in Brazil, as a means of punishing her as much as anything. But that she could stand, perhaps even welcomed. The only thing she couldn't take was if Scott tried to make love to her, tried to show her tenderness or affection. She wasn't sure why: perhaps because when he was gentle he was so like Mark, whereas when he was hard and cold the resemblance became only superficial again. Or perhaps because her emotions were so raw and battered that she just couldn't cope with any new problems. But she had to be absolutely sure.

Slowly Alexa said, 'Do you swear that you won't touch me? That you won't . . .' Her voice faltered before the derision in his face.

'That I won't force myself on you? That I won't lay claim to your body? Is that what you're trying to say?' Scott sneered. 'I've already told you, this marriage will be nothing but a formality.' The sneer deepened. 'Don't worry, Alexa, I'll leave you alone. You'll be able to lie in bed every night and fantasise to your heart's content about being with Mark!'

That declaration should have reassured her, and in a way Alexa supposed it did, because she was quite sure that he would keep his word, but somehow it also made her feel cheap and ugly. Made her feel as if she had to try and justify herself.

'That's a rotten thing to say!' she burst out. 'Can't you try to understand? I loved Mark; he was everything I had in the world. There had never been anyone else—and now there never will be. They say that people fall madly in love—well, I was! I was crazy about him. And then he—and then he just threw it all back in my face.'

Bitterness had come into her voice and she went to go on, but Scott interrupted her harshly. 'And so you decided to act the part of an injured martyr, even going so far as dying for your lost love. The final, supreme act of martyrdom. My God, Alexa, you disgust me!'

'But I loved him so much,' she protested feebly.

'All right, so you loved him. And Mark found that, although he was very fond of you, he felt more deeply about someone else. Or maybe he never really loved you at all, just felt coerced by the strength of your love into feeling that he ought to return it. It happens all the time; most couples have one partner who loves more deeply than the other.' Scott took a couple of steps into the room and stood looking down at her, his hands thrust into his pockets. Unmercifully he went on, 'If Mark hadn't met Elaine he would probably have married you and gone on for the rest of his life without knowing what real love was while you let your emotions feed off him like a leech. Mark was damn lucky that he met Elaine in time, because he would never have been really happy with you, and always would have felt that there was something missing from his life.'

Her face very pale, Alexa said tartly, 'And my feelings or what happens to me don't matter, I suppose.'

Scott frowned. 'Of course you matter. And you're entitled to feel hurt and sad. Even bitter and jealous—for a time. But if you're old enough to contemplate marrying someone, then you should also be old enough to face up to the fact that people can change their minds. And you've had time enough to put this behind you, Alexa. Okay, maybe it still hurts, but you must know that you're young and pretty enough to eventually meet someone else.'

'I don't want someone else,' she told him stubbornly. 'I only want Mark.'

Scott's face had lost some of its coldness while he had been talking to her, but now his features became withdrawn again. 'Then I feel sorry for you, because while you keep up that attitude you're going to miss out on everything there is to enjoy in life.'

Alexa lifted her head and looked at him bleakly. 'Mark was all that I ever wanted out of life. If I can't have him, then I don't care about anything else.'

For an instant anger glinted in Scott's eyes and he opened his mouth to argue with her further, but then he shrugged, muttered, 'What the hell's the use?' and turned disgustedly away.

CHAPTER THREE

THEY were married at the local Registrar's Office at nine o'clock on Friday morning. The ceremony took place in a small room that looked more like an office, with two women clerks acting as witnesses. The whole thing took less than ten minutes and afterwards Alexa couldn't remember a word of the promises they'd made. Not that it mattered—neither of them had any intention of keeping them anyway.

One of the clerks, seeing that she had no flowers to carry, had run out of the room and come back with a little posy of pink rosebuds, their ends wrapped in paper which gradually became wet from the vase of water which they had obviously been hurriedly taken from. It had been a kind gesture, but as they came out into the open again and stood on the pavement waiting for a taxi, Alexa looked down at them rather blankly. Bouquets were for brides, and she didn't feel at all like a bride. Her dream of being a bride had been at the old church in Seabrook, in a floating white dress with Mark at her side. But someone else had stolen her dream from her. A taxi drew up alongside and Scott opened the door and turned to help her in. Alexa looked round and saw that there was a metal litter bin attached to a nearby lamppost. Impassively she walked over and dropped the roses into it. Something flickered in Scott's face, but was quickly gone. She got into the taxi and they drove back to the flat to collect their luggage. Neither of them spoke. What was there to say?

The flight across the Atlantic to Rio de Janeiro was long and boring. For a time Alexa tried to watch the film, but the headset felt uncomfortable stuck in her ears and it seemed incongruous to sit among all these other people, the blinds drawn over the windows and the lights lowered to give the impression of being in a cinema, and yet know that you were in a great metal machine miles up in the sky. She settled back in her seat and closed her eyes, but it was too early to try to sleep and after a few minutes she moved restlessly and opened them again.

Scott turned his head to look at her; evidently he, too, wasn't finding much to interest him in the film. 'You okay?' he asked softly.

Alexa nodded and gave him a tight smile, then deliberately closed her eyes again so that she wouldn't have to talk to him.

During the last two days she had sunk back into numb apathy, letting him make all the arrangements and just doing what she was told. What did it matter if she married him? She told herself that nothing mattered any more. Only once did she even start to come out of it, and that was yesterday when she heard Scott speaking on the phone to his parents and she had the sudden fear that he was telling them about her, inviting them to the wedding. Without stopping to think, Alexa had rushed over and snatched the receiver out of his hand and slammed it down on the rest.

'No!' she shouted at him. 'I don't want them there. Do you understand? If you invite them I won't go through with it. I won't!'

Scott came angrily to his feet. 'Give me back that phone!'

'No! Not until you promise.' Alexa picked up the

instrument and clutched it to her, glaring at him defiantly.

Softly, menacingly, he repeated, 'Give me the phone, Alexa.'

She scowled at him, aware of the menace but not afraid enough to obey him. 'Have you told them about me? Have you invited them to the wedding?' she demanded.

For answer Scott merely reached out and silently took hold of one of her wrists, almost nonchalantly exerting his strength until she gasped and let go of the phone. He caught it before it could crash to the ground, then said grimly, 'Don't ever try anything like that again.'

Alexa stared at him, nursing her wrist which bore the red marks of his fingers. Mark had never once hurt her, would never have treated her like this. She looked down at her wrist and tears of self-pity pricked her eyelids. 'You hurt me!' she said indignantly.

'It's no more than you deserve,' Scott replied unfeelingly. He began to dial again and looked at her while he waited for the number to ring. 'I haven't told my parents. They know nothing about you coming with me. I was phoning them to say goodbye.'

'Oh. I—I'm sorry. I thought . . .'

But Scott had nodded dismissively and was speaking into the phone. 'Yes, we must have been cut off.'

The film ended, they were served with another meal by the hard-working cabin crew, and at last were told that they were coming in to land. Alexa glanced uninterestedly out of the window, only thankful that the long journey was over and she would be able to stretch her legs, but then she looked down through the clear sky and gave a little gasp of wonder as they came in over the sea and she saw the long, impossibly white beaches and the city streets penetrating like the fingers of a hand between the high, steep-sided green hills. Then she recognised the shape of Sugar Loaf Mountain, like the head of a giant, crouching lion guarding the entrance to the immense harbour. It was a view that she remembered seeing countless times in photographs, but somehow she had never imagined just how huge and awe inspiring it could be in reality.

The plane flew on, circling round and Scott leaned towards her, pointing, 'Look, over to the left.'

For a moment Alexa could see nothing but a bank of cloud below them, but then, soaring out of the cloud, she saw the top of a high mountain and on it, magnificent in its simplicity, a colossal statue of Jesus Christ. The statue's arms were outstretched in forgiveness and compassion as he gazed down at the huge city, His robes falling in swathed folds to His feet.

'That's Corcovado mountain,' Scott told her as she gazed down in awestruck wonder. 'The statue is about a hundred feet high.'

'How long has it been there?'

'Since 1931, I think. It was put up to celebrate Brazil's first century of political independence.'

'It looks a beautiful city,' Alexa remarked, showing the first signs of interest since she'd agreed to go with him.

'From the air it does,' Scott agreed rather grimly. 'But when you get on the ground you see all the *favelas*—the slum districts—climbing up the hillsides behind the new buildings.'

He pointed out Copacabana beach to her, away in the distance, but then the plane came in to land and she clutched the arms of her seat rather nervously as the ground came rushing up to meet them. Scott glanced at her and moved his hand as if to cover hers, but then changed his mind and began to talk to her instead, telling her about Rio. The plane landed, bounced, and then began to brake to a reasonable speed. Alexa let out her breath and realised that Scott was still talking to her.

'All right now?' he enquired.

She nodded and confessed nervously, 'I'm afraid I'm not very good on the take-offs and landings.'

She regretted saying it the instant the words were out of her mouth, expected him to take it as another example of her cowardice and to look at her derisively, but to her surprise Scott answered, 'Yes, flying does rather seem to consist of either extreme tension or extreme boredom.'

They gathered their things together and queued to leave the plane. As Alexa stepped out of the doorway she felt the heat hit her like a solid wave. The light was startlingly clear and intense and it was so hot that the surface of the tarmac shimmered in the sun. Everyone crowded into the bus for the short journey to the terminal and Alexa could feel herself beginning to perspire even before they reached the air-conditioned coolness of the building. They went through Customs and Alexa expected that they would collect their luggage and leave the building, had even begun to wonder mildly whether Scott had an apartment near one of those beautiful beaches, but instead he hurried her along to another terminal and produced tickets for a connecting flight.

Alexa looked at him in astonishment. 'I thought you lived in Rio?'

He tucked the boarding passes in his wallet and turned to look at her. 'I didn't say I did.'

'You didn't say you didn't, either,' Alexa retorted indignantly. 'Why didn't you tell me where you worked?'

'Because you were too busy feeling sorry for yourself to ask,' Scott pointed out sardonically. 'Come on, let's try and get a drink while we're waiting for the plane.'

Taking her arm, he piloted her through the throngs of people towards the Departure Lounge. It was very noisy; everyone seemed to be talking at the top of their voices, greeting friends ecstatically, calling out to one another, and the people were mostly dressed in bright, casual clothes. Alexa let herself be led through them rather bemusedly, realising how different the people were, getting her first view of the friendly, open Latin temperament.

It was quieter in the Departure Lounge, and she was glad to sit and sip the coffee Scott brought her. It was served black and was very strong and very sweet, a far cry from the instant she used to make at home.

'Do they always serve it like this?' she asked him.

'Why, don't you like it?'

Alexa sipped again experimentally. 'Yes, I do, actually. Or at least I think I could grow to like it.'

'That's rather the reaction one has to Brazil itself,' Scott remarked. 'At first everything seems very strange and alien, but then it gradually begins to grow on you until it takes a hold.'

'And has it—taken a hold on you?'

He nodded. 'Oh, yes. It happens to everyone, especially in the area where I work.'

'Just where *do* you work?'

His mouth twisted sardonically as Scott said, 'I wondered when you'd finally get round to asking that question.' Putting down his cup, he sat back in his chair and watched her reaction as he answered, 'I work in the Amazon Basin.'

Alexa frowned. 'The Amazon Basin? But that's mostly jungle, isn't it?'

'That's right. The company I work for is trying to reclaim the land and make it profitable.'

'But ... but ...' Memories of long-ago geography lessons were coming into her mind and Alexa was staring at him in growing horror. 'Surely the Amazon area is terribly wild and primitive? Full of snakes and alligators, and—and Indians?'

'There are all those things there, admittedly,' Scott replied calmly, 'but it isn't completely lacking in civilised amenities. The place we're going to is called Monte Dourado on the River Jari. It's a new town and probably one of the cleanest and best laid out in Brazil, except for the new capital of Brasilia.' He grinned rather sardonically. 'Don't worry, Alexa, you won't find any snakes in the bathroom.'

'I'm thankful to hear it. In fact I'm thankful to hear that there's a bathroom at all. I'd begun to envisage a mud hut in the jungle. What do you do in this place— Monte Dourado?'

She looked at him as she asked the question, saw his mouth twist again and realised exactly what he was thinking—that it was about time she'd got round to asking that question too.

He astounded her by saying, 'I'm a forestry expert. I help to clear the jungle and plant new trees that will be of benefit to the company or the community. You look surprised,' he added drily.

'I am,' she admitted. 'I thought—I don't know, I thought you'd work in an office in a city, like Mark.'

Scott's eyes narrowed. 'That isn't my scene. I'm not like Mark at all.'

Her eyes ran over his face, feature by feature. 'Except to look at,' she said slowly.

'That, perhaps. But in every other way we're completely different. And the sooner you realise that the better.'

'Oh, don't worry,' Alexa retorted bitterly, 'I know that already. Mark is twice the man that you'll ever be.'

Anger flashed in his grey eyes and his hand tightened on the cigarette lighter he was holding, but then it was gone and he carried on lighting his cigarette. 'That,' he replied calmly, 'is the kind of crack I'd expect from a lovesick adolescent. But that's just what you are, Alexa, a girl instead of a grown woman.'

For a moment she was annoyed and wanted to answer him back, but then it occurred to her that Mark, too, might have thought her naïve and immature. Was that why he'd preferred Elaine? she wondered desperately. Hadn't she been sophisticated enough for him? Had she been too open with her emotions, shown that she loved him too much? Misery filled her heart and was mirrored in her face, in the sadness in her eyes.

Scott stood up abruptly. 'You'll need something to read on the plane. Let's see if we can get any English magazines at the bookstall.'

The next plane was much smaller than the big jumbo on which they had crossed the Atlantic, and it was painted in the blue and white colours of Varig, a major Brazilian airline. It took them across country to the town of Belem, an old colonial port on the southern side of the River Amazon. By the time they got there Alexa was beginning to feel very tired, but it seemed that they still weren't at the end of their journey. They caught another plane, this time belonging to the company for which Scott worked.

'Why is it taking us across the sea?' Alexa demanded fretfully. 'I thought we were supposed to be going inland.'

Scott glanced past her out of the window. 'That isn't the sea, it's the River Amazon. It's over two hundred miles wide, so big that you can't see the banks.'

Alexa gazed down at the river, only now beginning to understand a little of the vastness of Brazil, a country which in itself was almost as big as the whole of the United States. That any river could be so big seemed impossible, especially to someone who'd been in the habit of taking their lunchtime sandwiches to the bank of the River Thames to sit looking across at the mass of buildings on the other side. A piece of land came into view and she thought they had crossed the river at last, but it was only an island that slipped past out of sight. At last water gave way to the rich green of equatorial rain forest that seemed to go on and on interminably. Alexa grew too tired to look out, turned her head away and fell asleep.

She slept on until the sound of the stewardess making an announcement made her stir and open her eyes. To her dismay, Alexa found that her head was pillowed against Scott's shoulder. Hastily she sat up and muttered an apology, putting up a hand to tidy her hair. Scott stretched his back as if he'd been sitting rather stiffly and she wondered how long she had been using him as a head rest. It was getting dark as they left the plane, but Alexa had no idea what the time was; she hadn't altered her watch after they had crossed the Atlantic and they had been travelling for so long that she felt completely disorientated—suffering from jet-lag, she supposed.

It was cooler now but still very warm, with that curious stillness in the air that you always seem to get in tropical countries. Alexa wearily let Scott walk her over to the lights of the airport buildings, longing for a bath and to go to bed. As they entered the main building, a man straightened up from where he had been leaning against the wall, waiting, and came towards them smiling broadly, hand outstretched. He was young, fair-haired, with a not unattractive beard covering his chin, giving an impression of tanned handsomeness.

'Scott—welcome back! Great to see you.' He wrung Scott's hand and laughed. 'And with a bride too, you old reprobate! I thought it was your brother's wedding you were going to. I could hardly believe it when they told me that you were married and wanted a bungalow!'

Scott grinned back at him. 'Well, you'd better believe it, because here she is.' His fingers tightened on her elbow and he drew her forward. 'Alexa, this is Tony Grant. Tony, my wife.'

Something in Scott's voice made her look at him sharply, but she could read nothing in his face. Perhaps it was just because he had called her his wife for the first time and they both knew how false the word was. Their eyes met briefly, but then his friend was claiming her attention.

'I'd always had Scott marked down as a confirmed bachelor. You must have really bowled him over—but I can see why,' he added gallantly. 'Welcome to Brazil, Alexa.'

'Th-thank you.'

He shook her hand vigorously and then helped Scott

to collect their luggage and carry it outside to a big American estate car. Alexa sat in the back of the car but was too tired to take in very much during the short drive from the airport. All she noticed was long lines of white bungalows set at regularly spaced intervals on either side of the straight roads, their lights shining out into the darkness. Tony was driving and soon pulled into the driveway of a bungalow that was all in darkness.

'Here's the key,' he said to Scott. 'Don't worry about your cases; I'll bring them.'

Scott opened the car door for her and they walked slowly up the driveway in the light of the headlamps. Alexa was aware of trees all around and the rich, spicy smell of vegetation, but then her thoughts came swiftly back to reality as Tony called out, 'Hey, don't forget you're supposed to carry the bride over the threshold!'

Scott turned the key in the lock and gave a slight shrug. 'I suppose we'd better keep up appearances.'

He stooped and lifted her easily, holding her securely within the strength of his arms. Alexa remembered the way he had picked her up and carried her to her bed on that black night of despair after Mark's wedding. He had saved her life then, brought her back from the edge of death almost by sheer willpower. And now they were thousands of miles away and were beginning to play out the farce of being married. She lifted her head to look into his face and was surprised for a moment to see a bleak look around his mouth, but then his eyes met hers and the look was quickly gone. He shoved open the door with his shoulder and carried her into the bungalow.

Immediately the place was flooded with light and a horde of people seemed to spring out of the darkness, laughing and calling out, pressing round them.

'Surprise, surprise!'

'Congratulations!'

'Hey, Scott, you old son of a gun, why didn't you tell us you were going home to get married?'

Scott's arms tightened, whether in astonishment or warning, Alexa didn't know, but then he set her down on her feet as all his friends, both men and women, crowded round, congratulating him, demanding to be introduced, shaking them both by the hand. They were nearly all in the same age group: from late twenties to early middle age, and all looked healthy, tanned and well—if casually—dressed. There were some other English accents there, but mostly the people seemed to be American or Brazilian. Scott introduced her to them all and she automatically smiled and shook hands, but was too tired and stunned by it all to take in many names. Somebody produced bottles of champagne and corks flew about, to the delight of the guests, who seemed to have had quite a few drinks already.

Tony yelled for silence and raised his glass. 'A toast to the bride and groom. Scott and Alexa.'

The words bride and groom had immediately brought that other wedding to her mind and Alexa grew tense and pale, but then a cheer went up and a woman's voice called out, 'Come on Scott, let's see you kiss the bride!'

'Yes, kiss the bride!' The cry was laughingly taken up on all sides.

Alexa stiffened and went to turn away, but found Scott's arm there, restraining her. 'No!' she muttered at him through gritted teeth.

'Don't be silly.' Putting an arm round her waist, he drew her firmly towards him even though she held herself in rigid defiance. Then his other hand came up to the back of her neck, forcing her to lift her head. His grey eyes looked into hers for a moment, and then he bent to kiss her.

Alexa kept her mouth firmly closed in angry resistance, but he didn't seem to care, his lips were hard against hers, exerting a sexual domination that could completely take over a woman if she ever gave it the opportunity. But Alexa remained frozen even though he kissed her for far longer than was necessary, while the cheers and whistles grew in volume.

At last he let her go and looked down at her enigmatically, noting the angry fire in her eyes, her flushed cheeks. He grinned sardonically and turned away as they all cheered again and yelled, 'Speech, speech!'

Scott said a few sentences, thanking them for the surprise party, adding a quip that made them all laugh uproariously again, but Alexa hardly heard him; she was still shaking with anger. Scott had no right to kiss her like that; to pretend was one thing, but there had been no pretence about that kiss—he had meant it. She wished fervently that the whole thing was over and that all the noisy, happy crowd of people would just go away. The talk became general again, she had a drink thrust into her hand and an American woman whose name she couldn't remember came over to her and started chatting animatedly.

'We had no idea that Scott was getting married. He really kept you a dark secret. He told everyone he was going home to be best man at his brother's wedding.'

'That was true,' Alexa said uncomfortably, wishing the woman would change the subject. 'His brother did get married.'

'And you two just up and decided to follow suit. Well, I'll be . . .'

'Yes, it all—er—happened very suddenly.'

'Say, did you make it a double wedding?'

'Oh, no,' Alexa assured her hastily. 'We were married quite some time after his brother.'

The woman looked puzzled. 'That must have been quite recently, then. When exactly did you get married?'

In the face of such a direct question, Alexa didn't have time to think that it might be a good idea to lie and blurted out simply, 'This morning.'

'This morning?' The American woman's already rather shrill voice rose several decibels. 'You mean to tell me that this is your wedding day? That this is your wedding *night*?' Before Alexa could answer the woman turned and called out above the hubbub of conversation, 'Hey, listen! Listen, everybody. I just found out that these two lovely people got married only this morning!'

'What? Hey, you're kidding!' The news was greeted with astonishment and Alexa found herself blushing as some people, women mostly, looked at her with speculative interest. Scott, she could see, was coming in for quite a bit of ribbing and double entendre from the men near him, but he seemed to be taking it all quite casually. He was standing over by the window, a glass in his hand, taller than any other man in the room, laughing at something Tony was saying to him. Alexa tried rather desperately to catch his eye as some women started asking her questions about the ceremony, about how long she'd known Scott, and, after a couple of minutes, he did in fact turn his head and look at her. Her eyes made unmistakable signals that she needed to be rescued, but to her chagrin, Scott merely raised his glass in a toast that might have been silent but loudly shouted the sheer irony of the whole thing.

Alexa's lips tightened and she interrupted the woman who was talking to her by abruptly asking to be shown the bathroom. She stayed inside as long as possible, seething with anger. Scott must surely have known that his colleagues would do something like this; he could at least have warned her. And added to being put at a disadvantage by surprise was the feeling that personally she didn't matter at all, the people were only interested in her because of Scott, as an interesting appendage that he'd brought back from England with him. They would probably have shown as much interest if he'd brought a pet dog instead, she decided bitterly.

When she went back into the living-room it was almost as if it was a signal for everyone to leave. But they didn't go without many demands to kiss the bride and giggling wishes of good luck.

Tony Grant was the last to go and looked rather embarrassed as he shook hands and said, 'I'm sorry, I wouldn't have arranged this if I'd known that—well, I expect you'd rather have been by yourselves tonight.' He realised that he was only making things worse, flushed, and at last took himself off.

The house seemed suddenly very quiet when they had gone. Scott drained his glass and set it down among several others on a small table. Alexa glared at him angrily and said, 'You might have come and rescued me! You knew I wanted you to. They were asking me all sorts of questions.'

'What about?'

'About how long we'd known each other, that sort of thing.'

'What did you tell them?'

'I tried *not* to tell them anything, but I gave the impression that we'd known each other for quite a long time. But for all I knew you could have been telling them exactly the opposite. You might have had the decency to warn me that they'd give a party for you—we could at least have worked out what we were going to say,' she added, her voice sounding waspish even to her own ears.

'The party was to welcome you as much as for me,' Scott reminded her evenly.

'That's hardly the impression I got, but I guess I'm supposed to clean up after it,' Alexa added, looking round at all the dirty glasses.

A harsh note came into Scott's voice. 'A maid will come in and do it in the morning. You won't have to lift a finger. You're tired,' he added abruptly. 'Why don't you go to bed?'

Her tone strained, Alexa answered coldly, 'I looked in the bedrooms; there's only one made up.'

His eyes rested on her for a moment before he said calmly, 'Then take it. I'll make up another in the spare room.'

She hesitated, then nodded and went to turn away, but something compelled her to look at him and ask with angry indignation, 'Why did you kiss me like that?'

Scott's eyes filled with mocking amusement. 'How did you expect me to kiss you?'

She was taken aback. 'Well—just a quick peck would have done.'

His eyebrows rose. 'My dear Alexa, you seem to forget that I have a reputation here to keep up. They all know that I can do a darn sight better than that!'

'Why, you—you . . .' Alexa glared at him in impotent rage, then stormed out of the room, slamming the door behind her.

She was so tired that she took little note of her

surroundings that night; it still hadn't really penetrated
that she was going to live here for the next few months
and the bungalow might just have been a suite in a
hotel. She undressed, showered, and made sure that
Scott wasn't around before slipping back into her
room and throwing herself exhaustedly into bed. All
she wanted was sleep, but perhaps she was overtired
because she lay awake for some time in the darkness
thinking, remembering those speculative looks some of
the women at the party had given her. Were they
wondering if this was the first time that she and Scott
would go to bed together? Or whether they had
anticipated the wedding ceremony? Alexa lay alone in
the big double bed and smiled thinly. If they only
knew! But then she remembered that she and Scott
had been together in bed once and had almost made
love. The smile faded as she recalled that night,
remembered how skilled and passionate he had been,
making her cry out with need and longing. Only her
need had been for Mark, not his brother.

She turned restlessly on the pillow. Scott had no
right to kiss her like that. He had promised that he
wouldn't touch her. It was all very well for him to say
that he had a reputation to keep up, but ... Her
thoughts froze suddenly. He had said that no single
women were allowed on the project, so all those
women at the party tonight must have been married.
So if Scott had a reputation here it must mean that
he'd had an affair with one of the wives. Possibly even
more than one. The looks the women had given her
suddenly took on a whole new meaning. Her eyes were
wide open now, staring into the darkness of the room.
God, was she supposed to live here with him while
Scott calmly carried on a love affair with his mistress
and/or mistresses? She could hardly expect him to

remain celibate for her sake, she supposed, but what kind of a position would it leave her in? Everyone would think that she was so unexciting in bed that he'd got tired of her almost immediately. Her mind tried to cope with the problem but sheer fatigue eventually overcame her and she fell into an angry sleep.

When she woke it was far on into the next day. For a moment she couldn't think where she was, but then that rich earthy smell drifted to her nostrils again and she sat up, fully awake. The air in the room was at a pleasant temperature, not too hot at all, and she realised that the gentle humming noise continuously in the background must be from an air-conditioning plant. She was more receptive to her surroundings now and looked around her with interest. The room was well, almost luxuriously, furnished, in a style she wasn't used to but recognised from films and television serials as upper class American. The plumbing in the bathroom, too, was all you would expect from a country that were reputed to be experts on the subject. Alexa wondered who had chosen the decor and whether all the bungalows were the same.

After she had dressed, she went into the sitting-room and felt a slight sense of anti-climax when she saw that Scott wasn't there. Perhaps he was still asleep? Slight sounds emanated from the kitchen, so she pushed open the door and went in.

A short, dark-haired woman was standing at the sink, cleaning vegetables. She swung round as Alexa entered and her olive-skinned face broke into a big smile as she gave a funny kind of bob. 'Good day, *senhora*. Good day. You want eat?'

Alexa blinked at her and then remembered that Scott had mentioned a maid and realised that the sitting-room had already been cleaned up while she slept.

'In a moment.' She shook her head. 'Er—my husband. Mr Kelsey. Do you know where he is?'

The maid's face broke into another big smile and she pointed outside. 'He in garden.'

'Thank you.' Alexa hesitated, looking at the other woman. Her face was very lined so it was hard to tell what age she was, possibly anything between twenty-five and fifty, and she was very thin and wiry. 'What is your name?' Alexa asked her.

Another beam. 'Maria. Maria Ramos.'

Alexa nodded and walked out into the garden. It occurred to her that Maria would know that she and Scott had slept in separate rooms. In a close-knit community like Monte Dourado all the maids probably gossiped to one another like mad, and it wouldn't be long before that titbit of news spread among all the guests who had been at last night's party. And just what would that do to Scott's reputation as a lover? she thought with grim satisfaction as she saw him sitting at a table in the shade of a tree, drinking coffee and studying some papers.

He looked up as she walked towards him and she said, 'Good morning,' in a tight, brittle voice.

'You're a bit late,' he informed her. 'It's nearly three in the afternoon.'

'Oh. I'll have to adjust my watch.' She sat down in a chair opposite him and looked around her. There were fences between their garden and its neighbours so that you had privacy, but the garden itself was very bare, just a large lawn with flower beds all round the edge. 'Why aren't there any trees and shrubs here?' she demanded.

'Snakes,' Scott replied laconically, and it suddenly came home to Alexa that she wasn't in some suburban American town but in the Amazon basin.

'Oh! I suppose the place is swarming with them?' she remarked, looking fearfully round and hastily lifting her legs off the ground and sitting on them.

Scott watched her in amusement. 'Absolutely swarming,' he agreed. 'You can't even drive your car over to the supermarket without running over a hundred or so.'

Alexa realised that she was being teased and glared at him. 'Is there really a supermarket?'

'Yes. And a hospital and a school and a sports complex. I told you, it's really very civilised here.'

Glowering at him antagonistically, she snapped, 'I suppose you think my being afraid of snakes is funny?'

Scott glanced at her, saw the tightness in her face, and sat back to give her his full attention. 'Real fear is never funny. But when you allow preconceived ideas to create a fear that isn't there . . .' he shrugged eloquently.

'Then that is funny,' she finished for him.

'For a while. Then it becomes boring.'

Alexa flushed, said stiffly, 'I'm sorry if I'm being a bore.'

'Don't be so damn touchy,' Scott replied brusquely. 'You may be immature, stupid, and a pain in the neck, but a woman with your looks would never become a bore to have around.'

Well! She'd been paid some compliments in her time, but never one as backhanded as that! And she wasn't sure that she liked what it implied. She started to say, 'Look, let's get one thing straight . . .' but Maria came out of the house carrying a tray with more coffee, together with crispy bread rolls, butter and a pot of marmalade, and she had time for second thoughts. Maybe now wasn't the time to force the issue.

'You were saying?' Scott queried when the maid had gone.

'Oh—nothing. What are you reading?'

'Reports on the planting programme. Just catching up on what's been happening while I was away.'

'You seem very keen on your work,' Alexa remarked rather wryly.

'I am. This Corporation is doing something really worthwhile here.'

He waited for her to ask him what it was and gave a thin-lipped smile when she didn't but said instead, 'They must be slavedrivers if they expect you to work on your first day back. Especially when they think it's the first day of your . . .' Alexa stopped, suddenly realising where she was heading.

'My honeymoon?' Scott supplied for her. 'On the contrary, they've been very understanding. I've already had a note sent round telling me to take a few more days off before I report back.'

Alexa concentrated on breaking open a roll and buttering it. 'And are you going to?'

He looked at her contemplatively. 'There would hardly seem to be much point, as ours isn't a real marriage.'

'But they're not to know that.'

'True,' he admitted. 'What do you think? Should I take the time off?'

Alexa looked at him in surprise; it was the first time he'd ever bothered to ask her opinion on any course of action. In London he had simple *told* her what they were going to do. She shrugged indifferently. 'I couldn't care less what you do. I certainly don't want you around, if that's what you mean?'

'That's exactly what I thought you'd say,' Scott told her. 'Which is why I went over to the office this morning while you were asleep and reported in.'

'Oh.' She hesitated a moment. 'Weren't they—surprised?'

'Extremely.'

Alexa looked at him in some annoyance, sure that he was being deliberately unhelpful. 'So what did you say to them?' she demanded.

'I merely told them that we'd decided to postpone our honeymoon until my contract here finishes and we go back to England.'

'And they accepted it?'

Scott shrugged. 'They had little choice.'

Thinking it over as she sipped her coffee, Alexa saw that he was right and that he could hardly have given any other explanation—not one that would prevent their spending the next few days alone together, at any rate. 'But it hardly fits in with keeping up appearances, does it?' she pointed out.

Scott raised his eyebrows in enquiry.

'Not taking time off for a honeymoon—it's hardly in keeping with the impression you tried to create last night at the party.'

'What impression was that?' he asked, his expression quite bland and innocent.

Alexa flushed, quite sure that he was secretly mocking her. 'You know darn well what I mean—when you kissed me, quite unnecessarily.'

His voice mild, Scott said, 'It seemed necessary at the time.'

'But you didn't have to do it as if you meant it!' Alexa snapped back at him.

He got lazily to his feet and stood looking down at her. 'You know, Alexa,' he remarked silkily, 'the way you keep going on about that kiss, anyone would think you wanted me to do it again.'

For a moment, Alexa was too taken aback to speak, could only sit and glare at him, but then she felt an overwhelming urge to hit back. Without bothering to think about the consequences, she retorted acidly, 'Well, that's just where you're wrong. No way do I want your kisses when I've experienced Mark's. As a lover you don't even make the first grade compared to him!'

CHAPTER FOUR

SCOTT'S expression hardly altered, but Alexa saw his jaw tighten and his eyes grow cold and knew that her barb had struck home. A feeling of triumph and power filled her, but it was short-lived; what was the point of fighting with Scott when they still had to try and survive together for the next four months? And just mentioning Mark's name had brought all the old pain tearing back into her heart. Dully now, she said, 'I'm sorry, I shouldn't have said that.'

He didn't answer, just stood looking down at her, and Alexa felt compelled to add, 'You goaded me. You know you did.'

'Yes,' he agreed unexpectedly, 'but even anger is a whole lot better than the apathetic state you were drifting into.' Reaching down, he took hold of her arm and hauled her to her feet. 'Come on. My boss has insisted that I take today off at least to show you around, so that's what we're going to do.'

Still holding her arm, he took her round to the front of the bungalow to where a white Range Rover type car stood in the driveway. Alexa noted that it had the number seventy-nine painted on the door but had no number-plates.

'First I'll show you round the town,' Scott told her as they got in.

Monte Dourado wasn't very large as modern towns go, but it was all beautifully laid out to a thoughtful, spacious design, the ground literally hacked out of the jungle.

'How long have they been building the town?' Alexa asked him for want of something to say.

'Since about 1970. About ten thousand people live here now, officially.'

'Mostly American and European?'

'No, by far the largest percentage of people who live and work here are Brazilians, which is as it should be. Admittedly the whole project was started by an American, but it's for the good of the Brazilian people, especially the very poor, as it creates a great many jobs.'

He went on telling her the history of the town and the area, at the same time pointing out to her places like the pig-breeding farm, slaughterhouse, and various processing plants. Alexa listened for a while, but there was only so much her eyes and brain could take in, and besides, tiredness was catching up with her and she had to lift a hand to cover a yawn.

Scott saw the action and said dryly, 'I apologise. I didn't realise it was that boring.'

'It's not,' Alexa said defensively, even though she hadn't been particularly interested. 'I'm just tired again, that's all, although I shouldn't be, because I slept for ages.'

'It's jet-lag. Your body-clock is all out of order. We'll go over to the apartment that I used to live in to collect my gear and then I'll take you back to the bungalow.' He turned the car and drove back the way they'd come, not bothering to talk to her now.

Alexa sat back in her seat and glanced across at his hard profile. She was aware that he was very enthusiastic about this project and that he wanted her to take an interest in it, but she really couldn't see what he was getting so worked up about. Okay, so they'd reclaimed some land from the jungle and built a

town. So what? Britain had been completely covered
in forest once, and look at it now. Maybe here the
transition was taking place far more quickly, but then
they had modern machinery and tools to help them.
And the town itself certainly wasn't anything to get
excited about. She yawned again and closed her eyes
against the sun.

'Here we are. Do you want to come in while I get
my stuff together?'

Scott's voice woke her from a doze and she
climbed rather stiffly out of the car. He had pulled
up outside a building of a not displeasing design,
insofar as any building built entirely of glass and
concrete can be said to be pleasing to the eye. The
car had been air-conditioned and stepping out of it
was like stepping literally under a sun-lamp, so that
she was glad to follow Scott through the glass door
into the cool interior of the apartment block. They
took the lift up to the second floor and he took a
key from his pocket and inserted it into the door of
number eight.

The flat was very neat and masculine with
everything tidied away and no unnecessary ornaments
on shelves or windowsills. The furniture, Alexa
guessed, came with the flat, as it had with the
bungalow, but Scott didn't seem to have impressed
much of his personality on it at all. Going into the
bedroom, he crossed over to the built-in wardrobe,
took out a suitcase and began to fill it with clothes.
Alexa looked round curiously for some indication of
his interests, but apart from a bookcase full of books,
and tennis and squash rackets standing over in the
corner, he seemed to have left little of himself in the
room. There weren't even any photographs. Curiously
she went over to the bookcase but found that most of

them were reference works on forestry, agriculture or
Brazil. Dull stuff.

She followed him into the bedroom, but here again
there were no photographs and few personal belongings.

'You travel lightly,' she remarked. 'Don't you have
any things of your own?'

'All the books and a couple of the pictures are mine.
But I don't believe in getting bogged down with
unnecessary possessions.'

'Is that why you never married? Do you see a wife
as an unnecessary possession?'

Scott's dark brows drew into a frown, but he merely
answered, 'I've never met any woman that I wanted to
give up my freedom for.'

Then Alexa remembered her theory about his
mistresses. No wonder he hadn't wanted to give up his
freedom when he could have sex without the ties of
marriage. She looked at the stripped bed, the covers
neatly folded at its head. Had he brought his women
here? Had he made love to them on its narrow
confines? Abruptly she turned away and said, 'But you
were willing to give up your freedom for Mark's sake.'

He stopped folding a shirt and turned to look at her.
'Mark's my brother.'

'You must care about him a lot if you'd marry
someone you didn't love for his sake.'

Scott finished folding the shirt; he did it neatly,
precisely, so that there would be few creases, and did
so with quick, practised movements as if he'd been
taking care of himself for a long time. When he had
finished he straightened up and answered, 'Of course I
care about him. He's my kid brother and I suppose it's
become a habit to watch out for him—I've been doing
it ever since I can remember. And as for marrying
you . . .' He paused, then said deliberately, 'It's no

great thing. It isn't as if you meant anything to me.'

'No, I suppose not,' Alexa agreed after a moment. 'But it could be awkward for you. What if you met another girl and wanted to marry her?'

'I'm hardly likely to meet anyone here.'

'No, but you could meet someone in England. And then it might be difficult to explain away a very short first marriage.'

Scott took the last few things out of a chest of drawers and put them in the case. 'That's my problem, not yours,' he told her briefly.

But Alexa persisted. 'No girl would believe that you only got married for your brother's sake. You don't look the type to offer yourself as a sacrificial lamb.'

'Don't I?'

'No, you're too big.'

He looked amused. 'Then I shall just have to be a sacrificial ox, shan't I?'

But Alexa hadn't meant it that way, she'd meant that his personality was too big, too self-assured and confident to let himself be used by another. And yet he had—quite willingly.

'Why don't you go and start packing up the books?' he suggested in what was clearly a command. 'You'll find some cardboard boxes in that cupboard near the front door.'

Alexa hesitated a moment, then shrugged and moved to obey him; clearly he didn't want to carry on the conversation and she didn't really care enough to pursue it.

It was raining when they had collected all his things together in the entrance to the block and were ready to take them out to the car, heavy rain that came straight down out of a suddenly black sky and bounced back off the dry ground.

'It won't last long,' Scott told her. 'We might as well wait here.'

He leant back against the wall and lit a cigarette, calmly waiting. The rain was warm; as Alexa peered out at it one or two spots caught her bare arm and she was surprised that it wasn't cold. To step out into it would be like stepping under a fierce but pleasant shower.

'Does it rain a lot here?' she asked.

'Almost every day; this area is known as the Equatorial rain forest. That's why everything grows so quickly.'

'But it isn't as hot as I expected it to be. I thought that all the places near the Equator would be absolutely scorching.'

'Everyone thinks that,' Scott agreed. 'But the average temperature here is only about eighty degrees Fahrenheit.'

They fell silent again, watching the rain, until Alexa glanced across at Scott's stern profile as he drew on the cigarette. It was strange, until yesterday she hadn't really thought about him as a person at all; it was only here, in his own environment, that she had even begun to look at him properly. Not that his face ever betrayed much of his feelings; there was an enigmatic quality about him, a feeling that he kept part of himself hidden away, that the part he showed to the world was merely a mask that concealed an internal force that he kept well under control. Only once had she seen that self-control snap, on the night they had met and he had been so angry with her.

The rain stopped quite suddenly and the sun came out. Humidity seemed to rise out of the ground in waves and Alexa immediately felt hot and sticky. They quickly piled the boxes and other things into the back of the car and drove back to the bungalow, grateful for the air-conditioning in the car. Alexa had an idea that she would spend most of her time in Brazil moving from one air-conditioning unit to the next, otherwise she'd just melt away.

They ate together that night, but Alexa was so tired that she went to bed immediately afterwards and didn't wake until she heard Maria moving around the following morning. Scott had already left; it seemed that work started early in Monte Dourado. She ate the breakfast that Maria had prepared for her, unpacked the last of her clothes, and then wondered what on earth she was supposed to do for the rest of the day. She tried talking to the maid, but Maria, although more than willing to stop work and chat, had a very limited English vocabulary and they soon had to fall back on sign language, which became a bit wearisome after a time.

Alexa smiled at the girl and indicated that she should get on with her work, then wandered out into the garden, keeping a wary eye out for snakes, giant spiders, or any of the other fearsome creatures she was quite sure crept out of the jungle. She tried to settle to reading a book, but soon grew restless and lonely. If Scott had been here she could at least have had someone to talk to. It occurred to her that she would have to depend on him a great deal during the next four months, and her mind filled with resentment. He had no right to bring her to this Godforsaken place where she couldn't even speak the language and then leave her alone all day with nothing to do. She dwelt on this all morning, letting the resentment build up, and instead of being pleased to have some company when Scott showed up at lunchtime, glared at him angrily instead.

He took one look at her face and said, 'Okay, out with it. What's on your mind?'

'I'm bored,' she told him baldly. 'There's nothing to do here. And I don't speak Spanish, so I can't even talk to Maria.'

Scott's mouth curled contemptuously. 'It wouldn't be much good if you did speak Spanish—they just happen to speak Portuguese in Brazil.'

'Really? I didn't know that,' she answered in surprise, momentarily diverted.

'It would have been easy enough to look it up. There are several books on Brazil among those we brought over yesterday. Anyone else would have been curious and eager to learn about the country they were living in. And even if you didn't feel like reading about it, you only had to ask.'

'I'm not interested,' Alexa retorted. 'And whatever language they speak, I was still left here all morning with nothing to do. And that's bad for me, isn't it?' she added spitefully. 'I might get depressed again and try to do something silly.'

The moment the words were out she wished them unsaid, especially when she saw the look of contempt deepen in Scott's eyes. She didn't like it when he looked at her like that.

'You obviously haven't read my note. I left it on the coffee table in the sitting-room.'

'A note? No, I didn't see it. What did it say?'

'Merely that I didn't want to wake you as you were still asleep, but I'd be back at twelve to collect you and take you to the Sports Club. I thought perhaps we could swim and then have lunch there.'

'Oh.' Alexa looked at him rather helplessly; the tone he'd used had been sarcastic in an offhand kind of way and it made her feel as she had when she was a child and had been shown up as having done something stupid. 'I'll—I'll get ready, then.'

She hurried into her bedroom to change into a sun-top and full, cotton skirt, and debated whether to take a one-piece swimsuit or a bikini, deciding in the end to play safe and take the one-piece. Scott was waiting for her when she came out. He ran his eyes over her but made no comment.

'Will this do for the Club?' she asked him uncertainly.

His eyebrows flickered in what she thought was amusement. 'Sure. Fine,' he agreed, but his answer only left her in doubt about whether he had found her clothes or her question funny.

The Sports Club was on the other side of Monte Dourado. It was spaciously laid out with tennis courts, both hard and grass, a huge swimming pool of Olympic proportions and a golf course that was still in the embryo stage. There was also a snack bar, a restaurant, and a couple of bars housed in white-painted buildings that had great masses of flowering creepers climbing up the walls and along the verandas in a riot of brilliant colours. It was Alexa's first experience of the exuberance of equatorial flowers and she gave an involuntary exclamation of delight, walking over to take a closer look as soon as Scott had parked the car.

'Good heavens!' she exclaimed. 'This whole bed is just one mass of orchids!'

'They grow wild here,' Scott informed her as he strolled up. 'There are over four thousand varieties of orchid in the Amazon valley, and as the climate is one long continuous summer they bloom all through the year.'

'How marvellous!' Alexa cupped her hands round

one exceptionally lovely bloom, its pale mauve petals flecked with purple and gold, and bent her head to drink in its scent. 'It's heavenly!' She lifted a glowing face to Scott, her eyes bemused by all the beauty around her.

An arrested look came into his grey eyes. 'You have pollen on your nose,' he told her, and lifted a finger to gently wipe away the golden dust.

Alexa laughed and his hand stilled. Her blue eyes came up to look into his and he watched the glow fade from her face, saw her eyes darken and look away.

Steadily he removed the last speck of dust and said, 'If you're that fond of flowers, you'll have to get some plants and put them in the garden of the bungalow.'

'But would it be worth it?' she objected, her voice not quite as calm as his. 'Surely they would take so long to grow that we'll have gone back to England before they come into flower.'

Scott shook his head. 'Plants grow unbelievably quickly here. It's like a gigantic greenhouse. You see that tree over there?' He pointed to a tree about ten feet high with large green leaves. 'How old do you think it is?'

Alexa leaned her head to one side as she contemplated it. 'Oh, I don't know. About four or five years old, I should think.'

Scott grinned. 'It's less than five months old. It's a gmelina; the tree that's been introduced here to take the place of the jungle growth.'

'Good heavens! It really grows that fast? Then they must grow to giant size in a few years?'

'They would, but we prune them back so that their trunks thicken out, but they still get up to about a hundred feet after ten years.'

As they talked they had been walking towards the

swimming pool and now half a dozen people sitting round a large table under a sun umbrella called out to them. 'Scott! Hey, over here!'

Scott acknowledged the shout with a wave, but led Alexa on to some buildings at the rear of the pool. 'You can change in there,' he indicated.

He was already in the pool when she came out; Alexa could see his dark head cutting through the water in a fast, strong crawl. She went in conservatively by the pool-wide steps at the shallow end and was surprised to find that the water was quite cool. After the humid heat of midday it felt just great. She wasn't a strong swimmer, but she enjoyed the water and was content to do a few widths of careful breast-stroke, putting a toe down to the bottom every now and again to make sure that she wasn't out of her depth. After about twenty minutes or so a head suddenly thrust up out of the water beside her and startled her so much that she forgot to swim and went under. A hand took hold of her arm and pulled her up, spluttering.

'Easy!' Scott held her by the arms and pulled her towards the shallow end until she found her feet.

Alexa wiped the water out of her eyes. 'You startled me!'

'Sorry. You about ready for lunch?'

'Yes.' He was very close. The water had plastered his hair to his head and trickles of it ran off the broad width of his shoulders down his arms and chest. A tight, constricting feeling came into Alexa's throat. She remembered once when she and Mark had taken a picnic down to the sea. They had found a small deserted stretch of beach that they had clambered to over the rocks, and Mark had insisted on bathing naked in the sea. He had wanted her to as well, but she had been shy and would only let him take off the top of her bikini. But he had kissed and caressed her and held her close against his wet chest. Hastily she turned away and waded towards the steps. 'I'll go and change.'

'No need. We can have lunch served to us by the pool and you'll soon dry off.'

Alexa picked up her towel and began to wipe herself.

'Here, I'll do your back.'

Scott went to take the towel from her, but she snatched it away, her eyes wide and dark with pain. 'Leave me alone! I don't need you,' she snapped at him.

He flinched back as if she really had tried to bite him, then a withdrawn look came into his eyes and he abruptly picked up his own towel, hooked it across his shoulders and strolled over to the group under the gaudy umbrella.

Alexa pretended to dry herself for another couple of minutes while she tried to recover some degree of poise, then went over to join them. She recognised them all as people who had been at the surprise party. As she crossed to the table she was aware of them watching her, the women in covert criticism of her figure in the wet, clinging bathing suit, the men probably wondering what she would be like in bed and whether she had been a virgin when Scott married her. Alexa walked tall under their scrutiny, a heightened colour in her cheeks.

As she came up, Scott deliberately put a casual arm across her shoulders and pressed warningly. 'You met all this crowd of reprobates at the party, if you remember.'

'Yes, of course,' Alexa smiled at them brightly. 'How are you all?'

Amid their greetings one of the women moved her chair round to make a space beside her. 'Come and join us.'

Someone brought her a chair and she sat next to the other girl, who was about twenty-eight, had short brown hair, freckles, and a friendly smile. 'I don't suppose you'll have remembered our names. Mine's Yvette Anderson,' the girl offered. 'And I'm married to Chris over there,' she added, pointing to a tall, fair, Nordic-looking man in his early thirties. 'How are you settling in?'

'Oh, fine. Scott drove me round the town yesterday. You seem to have everything you need here.' Alexa rather desperately sought for some topic of conversation.

'Sure. It's home from home,' Yvette drawled in her husky American accent, but there was a dryness in her tone that made Alexa look at her quickly and see the sympathetic twinkle in her eyes. 'We all found it strange and foreign at first. And you're very much a company wife. Maybe that's why all the English-speaking people tend to see a lot of one another. The wives are usually up here at the Club at least part of the day, when they're not visiting each other for coffee. We've organised ourselves tennis tournaments, squash and badminton championships, as well as a bridge club that meets every afternoon. Then in the evenings there are speakers who give lectures, although we've almost exhausted the supply of them, but we have debating groups, and at the weekends there are often dances here, or cocktails, or else we all go partying at somebody's house.'

'So at least you don't get bored,' Alexa said in some relief, the vision of spending all day alone at the bungalow receding fast.

'Gee, no,' Yvette said heartily. 'We're much too busy ever to get bored.' Her tone was even drier this time, but Alexa missed it. A waiter came up, everyone ordered lunch and the talk became general as they ate. Alexa gathered that this get-together was almost a daily ritual, the men starting work at about seven or eight in the morning, breaking off at twelve when the heat and humidity were at their highest, and then going back to work about three and working on until around six or seven in the evening. She also learnt, from their talk, that they all more or less lived in one another's pockets and knew everything there was to know about one another so that they had private jokes which no outsider would understand. Especially the men, as they also had their work in common. Whether there was any kind of hierarchy among the men, Alexa couldn't tell, but she gathered that forestry wasn't the only occupation at Jari, so perhaps they were employed in different jobs and there was no rivalry.

At three the men got up to go back to work and Scott came over to her. 'Would you like me to run you back to the bungalow?'

Yvette smiled up at him and said, 'You're not going to drag her away already, are you? We've only just started to get to know each other.' She turned to Alexa. 'Why don't you stay here for the rest of the afternoon? I can drop you off at your place on my way home.'

'Thanks, I'd like that.' She smiled gratefully and looked at Scott. 'I'll see you later, then?'

'Okay.' He lifted a casual hand in farewell and turned to go, but Yvette called him back.

'Hey,' she laughed, 'aren't you going to kiss your bride goodbye?'

'Of course.' He smiled crookedly and turned back. Alexa's mouth set into a stubborn line and her body tensed as he put a hand on either arm of her chair and leaned towards her. Then, to her surprise, he merely touched his lips fleetingly against her forehead. 'Goodbye, darling,' his voice heavy with an irony that was lost on everyone else.

He went off with the other men to change, and Alexa watched him go. Of the four of them Scott had by far the most athletic figure, his width was all muscle, and the planes of his stomach were completely taut and flat, whereas the Americans, in their brightly patterned swimming shorts instead of trunks, were already starting to thicken round the waistline and had the beginnings of a paunch. But then they were married, Alexa thought cynically, maybe they didn't get as much exercise as Scott did.

As they neared the building that housed the changing rooms, the men stood aside to let a woman come out of the door. Alexa saw them greet her and stand talking for a moment or two, and then the three other men went on in, but Scott and the woman stayed together, moving a few steps away from the path until they were partly hidden in the dappled shade of a palm tree. The woman was very tall and slim with blonde hair drawn back from her head and tied in a casual knot. She was wearing very short shorts that emphasised the length of her tanned legs, and a rich cream, shortsleeved shirt, hanging loose over her waist. She could have looked sloppy, but even from that distance it was obvious that the clothes were well-cut and expensive, and that, together with her high-heeled sandals and sunglasses, made her look instead casually elegant—a look that Alexa had often longed to achieve for herself. The two of them were standing close together, almost touching, and were talking earnestly.

'Yvette,' Alexa said on sudden impulse, 'that woman that Scott's talking to over there; I don't remember seeing her at the party.'

Yvette turned to follow her gaze and a flush of embarrassment spread across her face. 'Oh. No, she wasn't there,' she answered stiffly.

As Alexa looked across at the two of them again, the woman put a hand on Scott's bare chest in a gesture that was as intimate as a caress—and Scott raised his own hand to cover hers.

'Who is she?' Alexa demanded abruptly as she turned away, feeling rather like a voyeur and sure in her own mind that she had found Scott's mistress.

Yvette, too, seemed glad to turn her back on the couple. 'Her name's Patti Jordan. She lives in a bungalow not far from yours.'

How convenient! Alexa thought wryly. Yvette's voice still sounded embarrassed and Alexa felt rather sorry for her; it couldn't be a very nice situation when you had to tell a bride of a few days about her husband's former mistress! But even though she felt sympathetic Alexa just had to ask, 'Is she married?'

'Oh, yes. Her husband works with mine down at the pulp mill. They have what's known nowadays as a free and open marriage. In other words, neither of them feels any guilt when they have affairs. It wouldn't surprise me if they didn't enjoy telling one another all about them,' Yvette said rather bitterly, adding, 'You should watch out for her, Alexa.'

'Don't the people in charge here look down on that kind of thing?' Alexa asked, remembering the rule about no single women.

'Normally they do. But unfortunately Patti is the

exception. She's too important to them.'

Eyebrows going up in surprise, Alexa queried, 'Really? How come?'

'She's a scientist. A professor of something or other, and an expert on the processing of wood into its various by-products. I understand she's doing some kind of important research work, but it's all kept pretty quiet in case some rival company gets hold of the idea. It was she whom the Jari project wanted to employ; they just took her husband as part of the deal.'

'I see.' So the woman not only had beauty and obvious sex appeal but brains to go with it. Sometimes, Alexa decided, fate was very unfair with its hand-outs. Although she'd once thought that she was quite good-looking, better than Elaine at any rate, but Mark had preferred the other girl and now she had no confidence in her looks or anything about herself any more. She glanced across the pool again, but both Scott and Patti Jordan had gone.

The rest of the afternoon she spent at the Club, meeting more wives, swimming again and having her first bridge lesson. At five-thirty Yvette drove her home and dropped her outside the bungalow.

'You'll have to get Scott to buy you a car so that you can get around,' she remarked.

'No good, I'm afraid. I don't drive.'

'Well, I'm sure Scott would love to teach you. 'Bye!'

It would be fun to learn, Alexa decided, but she was quite sure there was nothing that Scott would like to do less than have to spend hours alone with her while she crunched through the gears of his car.

She thought she'd better check that Maria had the dinner in hand, but from the surprised look on the maid's face she realised that her concern was quite unnecessary, so she went away to wash her hair and change into a cool, sleeveless dress in her favourite deep red colour. Scott came in shortly after six and she could hear him whistling in the shower. Maybe he was happy at seeing his mistress again, Alexa thought bitterly. Perhaps they had even spent the afternoon together, unable to wait to make love after being apart for two weeks. Did they go to Patti's bungalow? she wondered. Or had they come here, to Scott's room?

Going out-into the corridor, she stood undecidedly outside Scott's door, her curiosity to see if his bed was rumpled almost overwhelming. She started to lift her hand to the knob, but just then the bathroom door opened and he came out, wearing a dark-blue bathrobe with his initials embroidered on the pocket.

'You sound very happy,' Alexa said accusingly to cover her relief at not being caught out.

His left eyebrow rose at her tone. 'Just because you're having a lovely time being miserable it doesn't mean that everyone else has to do the same, does it?'

'I don't—enjoy it.'

'No? Amazing how one can get the wrong impression, isn't it?' he jeered maddeningly. Alexa glared at him and flounced into the sitting-room.

His note was still on the coffee table where he had left it that morning. Angrily Alexa opened it and found that he had quoted it almost verbatim. He said that she was still asleep and she wondered if he'd looked in on her, the thought filling her with unease. She must remember tonight to look and see if there was a lock on her door.

The food that Maria had cooked was excellent, although rather spicy for Alexa's conservative English palate. She would gladly have eaten in silence, but

Scott kept asking her questions so that she had to tell him about her afternoon at the Club.

'Did you enjoy it?' he asked her.

'Yes, of course.'

'Good. I'd hate to think of you being bored.'

Alexa's face tightened at the irony in his tone. 'I'm bound to feel lonely in a foreign country when you're at work.'

'Lonely, perhaps. But you don't have to be bored.'

'They're one and the same, surely?'

'Not necessarily. It's possible to be self-sufficient within yourself. To create your own interests and amusements so that you're not dependent on other people.'

'Sit at home and read all day, do you mean?' Alexa asked disparagingly.

'If you find a subject that interests you enough. There are plenty of new things here that could hold your interest; how the Brazilians live, for example, or how the work we're doing here is affecting the Amazon valley and opening it up for more people to come here.'

Alexa wrinkled her nose. 'It sounds dull stuff.'

Scott looked at her for a moment, then back to his food. He was silent until he had finished, then sat back and said deliberately, 'I wrote to my people today. I told them that we'd married.'

'Oh, no!' She gazed at him in horror.

'They had to be told, Alexa. It isn't something we can keep secret.'

'Yes, we could. You didn't *have* to tell them.'

Scott shrugged impatiently. 'You're behaving like a child. My parents care about you and will be pleased to hear that you're with me.'

'I don't give a damn what your parents think!' Alexa

stood up so suddenly that she jolted the table and knocked over her glass, the wine spreading in a pink pool across the tablecloth. 'But they'll tell Mark! Do you understand—they'll tell Mark?'

Scott, too, got to his feet, his face hardening. 'So what? He had to know some time.'

'No, he didn't.' Alexa's voice rose hysterically. 'You did this on purpose! You promised you wouldn't tell them.'

'I promised I wouldn't tell them before the wedding; I didn't say anything about not telling them when it was over. Be sensible, Alexa. We . . .'

'No! No, I won't be sensible,' she burst out furiously. 'You did this deliberately. You *wanted* Mark to know that we were married so that he'd never feel guilty about me again—no matter what I did. You're just safeguarding him in case I—in case I . . .' She didn't finish the sentence, she had no need to. Her face filled with torment and there was despair in her voice as she said brokenly, 'All you care about is Mark. You don't give a damn about me.'

'Why the hell should I?' His cold bluntness made her lift her head and stare at him. 'You're behaving like a spoilt brat who's had her favourite toy taken away from her. Why should anyone care about you when you're so busy feeling sorry for yourself?' Brutally he added, 'Mark doesn't love you, Alexa. Perhaps he never did. He probably only fancied you a great deal and when that wore off he was just left with a girl with a pretty face and a good figure. But by that time you were so besotted with him and had made it plain that you weren't going to let go that he felt compelled to offer to marry you. I remember, he once mentioned in one of his letters that you were the clinging vine type,' he went on cruelly.

'Why, you—you . . .' Alexa's hands scrabbled among the things on the table. They closed round a heavy glass dish that had contained pats of butter and threw it at him with all her force. Scott ducked and the dish shattered against the wall. Looking round, he observed the scar in the plaster and to her fury began to laugh.

'You pig! You rotten egotistical swine!' Plates, the salt cellar and a jug followed the dish as fast as she could throw them. Scott dodged skilfully out of the way, his laughter increasing in ratio to her rage. Then he took a quick pace towards her and grabbed her wrist before she could hurl a fat, juicy paw-paw at him.

'You wild-tempered little bitch!' Deftly he twisted her wrist and caught the fruit before it could squelch on to the floor. 'You know, Alexa,' he told her, the laughter still in his voice, 'you really should improve your aim before you start using me as a coconut-shy.'

'You big slob!' She tried to free herself, but his grip tightened like a vice and he only laughed at her struggles. 'Oh God, how I hate you!' she stormed in impotent rage.

Scott opened his mouth to say something, but just then the door opened and Maria came in. She took one look at the broken china scattered around the floor, her eyes opened unbelievably wide in amazement and then she broke into a long, voluble and highly excited torrent of Portuguese. When she at last paused for breath, Scott answered her in the same language and they carried on a conversation for a couple of minutes before he turned back to Alexa. He had kept hold of her wrist and the amused mockery was back in his eyes.

'Maria wanted to know what had happened, so I told her we'd had a lovers' quarrel.'

'Really?' Alexa answered stiffly. 'Wasn't she surprised?'

'Oh, no. People of Latin America often have impulsive arguments. But she insists that we make it up at once; she says that it's unlucky to walk away from a quarrel without a smile.'

'Well, I have no intention of making it up,' Alexa retorted stonily.

Scott sighed theatrically. 'Well, if you won't, then I suppose I must.'

He moved a little nearer and Alexa looked at him in alarm. She was beginning to recognise that look in his eyes. 'Let go my wrist! You keep away from me!'

'But Maria insists,' he said silkily, and suddenly jerked her wrist forwards so that she fell against him. The next moment his other hand was behind her head and his lips were on hers, hard and forceful, not caring whether she responded or not.

Alexa tried to squirm away, but he took his time over it before he eventually let her go. His cool grey eyes met her flamingly angry blue ones for a moment, but then he turned to Maria, who was smiling and nodding happily, sure that her intervention had made them make up their quarrel.

'You'd better smile at her,' Scott said softly, 'or she won't be satisfied until we do it again.'

Alexa hastily gave a big grin and Maria clapped her hands several times before she became practical again and went out to the kitchen to get a brush to sweep up the broken china.

'Let's leave her to it and go and have our coffee in the sitting-room,' Scott suggested, firmly keeping hold of her hand so that she couldn't go and shut herself in her bedroom.

'I suppose by tomorrow it will be all over the town that we quarrelled,' Alexa observed bitterly.

'Does it worry you?'

She tossed her head. 'No, why should it? They probably already know that we don't share a bed anyway.'

'I shouldn't think so. The Brazilians are used to foreigners having funny ways. And I dare say we're not the only couple in Monte Dourado who sleep in separate rooms.'

He sounded as if he was pretty sure about it, and Alexa wondered whether Patti Jordan and her husband's open marriage extended to having separate bedrooms.

'If I let go of you will you promise not to start throwing coffee cups at me?' Scott asked her, only half jesting.

'Given a choice I'd rather throw the coffee pot!' she replied with venom.

'Temper, temper!' But he let go of her hand so that she could step away and throw herself down moodily on the settee. Scott moved to pour out the coffee and brought a cup over to her. 'Snap out of it, Alexa. The worst that Mark will think is that you married me on the rebound.'

'He might not. He might suspect the truth. After all, he does know me rather well,' she pointed out tartly.

'So what if he does? What Mark thinks of you can hardly matter to you now.'

'Of course it matters,' Alexa snapped back. 'I love him.'

He looked at her with an expression that was a mixture of curiosity and distaste, almost as if she was an exhibit in a freak show. 'Haven't you got any pride, Alexa?'

'Not where Mark's concerned, no. There's no room for pride in love.'

Scott sat back in his chair and laughed derisively, the sound far more eloquently describing his opinion than any words could have done.

Putting down her untasted coffee, Alexa stood up and faced him, her hands balled into tight fists. 'You don't understand because you don't know what it feels like to be in love with someone who doesn't love you! You just don't know.'

'Oh, yes, I do,' he answered harshly. 'I know exactly how it feels.'

Her eyes widened and she stared at him in surprise, seeing the grimness in his face and the way he gripped the arms of his chair until the knuckles showed white. She lifted one hand towards him in an impulsive gesture, then shrugged helplessly and ran out of the room.

CHAPTER FIVE

THEIR life at Monte Dourado began to fall into a pattern which, for Alexa, was simply the pursuit of whatever pleasure she could find in her state of mind. With Yvette Anderson as her mentor, she met and became friendly with most of the other wives and would spend most of her days at the Sports Club. She played tennis early in the morning before it became too hot, swam, and then played bridge or some other card game at a table near the pool in the afternoon or inside on the frequent occasions when the rain fell. Scott joined her for lunch most days, but sometimes he had to be away for a whole day when he visited the sites some distance away where the jungle was being cleared. In the evenings they would go for a drink or to watch a film show at the Club, or else they would be invited to some other couple's house to dinner or a cocktail party; seldom did they spend an evening at home alone together, both of them, by tacit consent, seeking the company of others.

During the first few weeks Alexa enjoyed herself; it was fun, after having worked ever since she left school, to call her time her own and be able to do what she wanted. And it was nice to learn new things and to be treated as an equal by women who were generally older and more experienced than she was. It was also a good panacea to have her days filled with new interests and new people so that she didn't have time to think too much of Mark and Elaine, of what they were doing now and whether Mark ever thought about her.

After they had been there about three weeks, Scott
one day casually tossed an air-mail envelope
addressed to Mrs S. Kelsey across the table to her.
Alexa looked at it for a long moment. When she had
been engaged to Mark it had thrilled her to think that
she would one day be Mrs Kelsey, but now she never
thought of herself as that and used the name as seldom
as possible. Luckily everybody at the Club was on first
name terms immediately they were introduced. Slowly
she put out a hand to pick up the envelope. She didn't
recognise the writing, but it bore an English stamp.

Scott, watching her hesitation, said dryly, 'You
needn't be afraid; it won't explode in your face. It's
from my mother.'

'Oh.' She toyed with it, turning the envelope in her
hands. 'I'll open it later.'

'Suit yourself.'

Scott went off to work and Yvette called round to
pick her up shortly after, so Alexa didn't open the
letter until she got home that evening and was alone in
her bedroom, and even then she did so very
reluctantly. It was a very kind letter, written by a
woman who didn't understand the circumstances and
probably wasn't at all happy about them, but was
determined to do her best to welcome her new
daughter-in-law into the family for her eldest son's
sake. She said how unhappy she had been when Mark
broke off the engagement and so how glad she was
now that Alexa had fallen in love with Scott instead. If
she only knew, Alexa thought bitterly, but she felt silly
tears pricking at the backs of her eyes. Scott's mother
went on to say how surprised and thrilled Mark and
Elaine had been to hear the news, and Elaine had said
she was going to write soon.

Alexa's face grew white as she read that last bit; the

last thing she wanted was to have Elaine writing to wish her happiness and to ask all the details of her marriage. Even less did she want to hear about Mark and Elaine's honeymoon and setting up house and how happy they were. A surge of hatred for Scott for having revealed their secret ran through her, and she petulantly threw the letter aside and slammed into the bathroom. She came out, wearing just a lacy bra and pants, just as Scott was walking towards his bedroom.

'My God, isn't there any privacy about this damn place?' she snapped at him.

His left eyebrow rose in the sardonic way she hated. 'What the hell's got into you?'

'You! You're what's got into me.' Alexa's voice rose, her anger fanned by the way his eyes went over her, lingering on her tanned figure and the almost see-through undies. 'I wish I'd never set eyes on you!'

She strode into her room and slammed the door shut in his face, but the next second he pushed it open and sent it crashing back against the wall.

'Don't ever do that again,' he ordered grimly. 'And don't try locking me out either, or I'll just kick it open,' he added, seeing her chin rise in mutinous defiance.

For a long moment they faced each other, but Alexa was the first to drop her eyes and turn away. With trembling fingers she picked up a robe and slipped it on, knotting it around her waist, trimmer now than it had been after playing so much tennis.

'Now,' Scott said grimly, 'perhaps you'll tell me what all this is about?'

'It's nothing,' she answered stiltedly. 'Please go away so that I can dress.'

'I've seen you without clothes before,' he reminded her jeeringly. Then, looking round the room, he saw the scattered sheets of the letter on the floor. 'So it was my mother's letter that upset you?'

'No, not really,' Alexa admitted honestly. 'It was something she wrote.' Scott waited in expectant silence and she said in a small, dull tone, 'She said she'd told Mark. And that Elaine would be writing to me.'

Crossing to her side, Scott took hold of her arm, pushed her down on the bed and sat down beside her. 'Is that so bad?'

'Oh, yes! Can't you see!' Alexa raised agonised eyes to his. 'Elaine will tell me all about the two of them, where they're living, what they've been doing. And I just can't bear to hear that. Can't you understand? I couldn't bear it!'

'So don't read her letter,' Scott commanded brusquely. 'Just tear it up. It's as simple as that.'

She looked at him in surprise. 'But surely—you'd look on that as the easy way out; the coward's way?'

'Of course I do.' He gave a slight shrug. 'But then you are a coward, aren't you? You've been taking the easy way out ever since you got here.'

Frowning, she said, 'I don't know what you mean?'

'Don't you? No, I don't suppose you do.' He got to his feet. 'Think about it. When you get the answer maybe you'll have taken the first step towards becoming an adult.'

Once a month they held a dance at the Club; it was treated as a big social occasion that most people attended and everyone dressed up for. Alexa had a couple of evening dresses in her wardrobe and put on a deep turquoise blue one with a strapless top and full skirt with an irregular, fringed hem. The colour suited her and she knew she looked good in it because Mark had told her so. Mark; why did everything make her think of Mark? The promised letter from Elaine hadn't yet arrived, but every morning she waited in trepidation for Scott to pass it to her, and only began to enjoy the day when he didn't.

What she'd learned to call 'the crowd', the Andersons and four or five other British or American couples, were already at the Club when they arrived. They had got one big table to themselves and the drink was already flowing, with all the men taking it in turns to buy a round. Tony Grant, Alexa noticed, was also there with several other lone men. They greeted the others and sat around and talked for a while, the women chattering away as if they hadn't seen each other for weeks even though they had spent most of the day together earlier. Scott joined in for a while, then excused himself and went over to talk to Tony and the other men. Alexa realised that until he had married her he had probably spent most of his time with the other bachelors and hadn't been part of the crowd at all, and she wondered whether he in any way resented his loss of freedom. If he did he was disguising it very well.

The band was a good one, it played all the latest hit tunes from America as well as more swingy numbers for the many Brazilian people there. Alexa had always loved dancing and her foot automatically beat time with the music. The other couples got up to dance to a particularly groovy beat and Alexa felt the loneliness that only a girl who is sitting out alone can feel. She looked impatiently across the room for Scott, wanting him to come back to at least sit beside her and not make her isolation so obvious, but the group of men had moved out to one of the bars. Alexa bit her lip then gave a gay smile as some of the crowd danced by and waved to her. Picking up her bag, she went out to

the cloakroom to powder her nose. When she got back
ten minutes later the beat had changed to a slow
number and she was just in time to see Scott walk on
to the floor with Patti Jordan.

For a few seconds she was taken by surprise, and
then felt a strange stirring of envy all mixed up with
anger and frustration as she watched Scott gather the
other girl into his arms, holding her close and smiling
down at her as she lifted a hand to the back of his neck
and leaned against him, her body in a long, clinging
white sheath of silk rubbing against his every time
they moved.

The bitch! Alexa thought fiercely. What's she
trying to do? Commit rape in the middle of the
dance floor? And that dress—she might just as well
not have bothered to wear one at all. It certainly
reveals a whole lot more than it hides. And how
dare Scott let her make a fool of him like that?
Couldn't he see that the woman was just using him
to show herself off? Or was he so much in love with
her that he was too blind to notice—or even to care
if he did? Then Alexa remembered that he had told
her that he, too, knew what it was like to love
someone who didn't love him back, and she decided
that it could only be Patti Jordan, and at once her
feelings changed. She no longer felt angry but
terribly sad; sad for all those people who never have
their love fulfilled.

'Alexa?'

She became aware of Yvette, who had come up to
her and was looking at her anxiously. She realised that
she must have been standing staring at the dancing
couple for several minutes and that Yvette was
worried about her, so she lifted her head, gave a bright
smile, and said, 'I was just watching Scott dancing

with Mrs Jordan. They make an attractive couple, don't they?' And then she walked, head still high, over to their table, leaving Yvette to follow her with a dumbstruck look on her face.

There fell a curious, expectant kind of hush round the table as she sat down, but Alexa smiled happily and turned to talk animatedly with the girl next to her and the uncomfortable moment was glossed over. A short time later she felt a touch on her shoulder and found Tony Grant standing beside her.

'Care to dance, Alexa?'

'I'd love to.' Tony took her on to the floor and held her loose and comfortably. For a moment Alexa toyed with the idea of flirting with him, but dismissed it almost at once; there would already be enough gossip without adding to it. And besides, Tony wasn't the type to flirt with his best friend's wife. He had probably only asked her to dance because he had been shocked by Scott's callous behaviour towards his new bride and had felt sorry for her. She guessed that Tony was like that; always kind to animals, children and neglected women.

'Tony, were you ever a Boy Scout?' she asked him.

He looked surprised but answered readily, 'Why, yes, I was. As a matter of fact I was even a Scoutmaster before I left England to come out here. Why do you ask?'

'No reason, really. I just thought you might have been.'

Tony grinned, in no way put out. 'You're comparing me to Scott. He isn't the Boy Scout type at all.'

Alexa glanced across to where she could see her husband's dark head close to Patti Jordan's blonde one. 'No, he isn't, is he?' she answered slowly.

'Look,' Tony began uncomfortably, 'Scott has known Patti for quite a while and . . .'

'Oh, I know,' Alexa interrupted with a bright smile. 'And I'm sure they have a great deal to catch up on. I know very little about the technical side of his job, so I'm very glad Scott has friends he can discuss his work with.'

Dawning admiration showed in Tony's eyes and there was something like respect in his voice as he said, 'You know, Alexa, maybe you are the right girl for Scott. Or at least you could be if you . . .' But then he broke off without finishing that intriguing sentence.

'If I what?'

'Oh, it doesn't matter. I guess it's something that you just have to find out for yourself. But of course you're the right girl for him,' he added hastily, recognising his faux pas.

The music ended then and he walked her back to her seat. Half-way there they almost bumped into Scott and Patti Jordan. They all four stood still, looking at one another, then Scott said easily, 'Patti, I don't think you've met my wife. Alexa, this is Patti Jordan, who's engaged in research work here at Jari.'

Alexa turned to the other girl and found herself being looked over by a pair of large hazel eyes that held cool curiosity. Thrusting out a hand, Alexa gave the blonde girl a big smile and said, 'How do you do, Mrs Jordan. I've heard so much about you.'

Her eyes lit with amusement and there was genuineness in her laugh as Patti Jordan took her hand and shook it. 'I'm quite sure you have, but I hope you won't let it prejudice you too much!'

For a minute Alexa thought she was being talked down to, but then she, too, grinned and answered, 'I'll try not to.'

They parted then, Scott taking Patti back, presumably to her husband, while Tony walked Alexa to her table. There she had the satisfaction of Tony hooking up a spare chair and sitting next to her, and Scott came back within a minute and took his place again at her other side.

Tony started asking Alexa about England, Scott joined in and the three of them chatted until the supper interval when Tony rejoined his friends and they ate with the rest of the crowd. After supper a couple of the Americans asked her to dance and Scott danced with their wives, then there came another time while everyone else was dancing and they were alone at the table.

They sat silently until Alexa felt compelled to say, 'Don't you think it will look odd if we don't dance together?'

'Possibly,' Scott agreed. 'But I didn't want to run the risk of upsetting you.'

'Why should it upset me?' Alexa asked slowly, guessing from the tone of his voice that he was playing with her.

'Because your feelings are so sensitive,' he explained in mocking seriousness. 'If I danced with you you'd only be reminded of the last time we danced together. On Mark and Elaine's wedding day,' he supplied as she turned her head to gaze at him.

Colour flooded through her cheeks and for a second she felt so angry that she could have hit him, but then she realised that he was purposely goading her and she bit back the retort that came to her lips. Slowly she shook her head. 'I don't think it would have reminded me of that. And I wouldn't have got upset if it had. If you don't mind, I would like to dance. Please.'

A frown of puzzlement replaced the mockery in

Scott's eyes, then he stood up and pulled her chair back. 'Of course.'

They danced very decorously. Scott didn't attempt to hold her close as he had Patti, and when the beat picked up he readily let her go so that they could move freely to the music, a good yard of space between them. He danced with her a couple more times and at about midnight suggested they leave, although the dance wasn't ended. Alexa agreed willingly enough; she wasn't tired, but she felt that she'd had enough of keeping up appearances.

Scott opened all the car windows as they drove home through the warm darkness. Occasionally, from the jungle, there came harsh cries and strange sounds, but it was far enough away for the noises not to jar or penetrate. It must have rained recently, because the air was redolent with humid sweetness. By now Alexa was used to the warmth of the nights and could hardly believe it when someone told her that they sometimes had frost. Scott was smoking a cigarette and she could see the end brighten and glow as he pulled on it. Impulsively she said, 'Will you teach me how to drive?' Adding hastily, 'You can buy cars here, can't you? I'd only want a small one and I have enough money to . . .'

He interrupted her brusquely. 'Of course I'll teach you. And you don't have to worry about a car. I can probably hire one for you for the rest of the time we'll be here.' He paused to pull on his cigarette again. 'Why the sudden decision?'

Alexa shrugged. 'I don't know. I just thought I might as well take advantage of the opportunity.'

At the bungalow she walked ahead of him into the sitting-room. Usually when they got home after an evening out she said goodnight and immediately went to her room, but tonight she lingered, throwing her evening bag down on to a chair but moving restlessly about the room, fidgeting with cushions and things.

Scott watched her for a couple of minutes and then moved over to the drinks tray. 'How about a nightcap?'

'Yes, please. Gin and tonic.'

He poured out the drink and brought the glass over to her. 'I do know what you drink by now,' he reminded her.

'Oh. Yes, of course.' She swirled the liquid in the glass, watching the ice clinking against the sides. 'Scott,' she began tentatively, 'I'd like to talk to you.'

He sat down in an armchair, his long legs stretched out in front of him, looking casually at ease even though he was still wearing his white evening jacket and black velvet bow tie. It was strange, she thought, how much a stranger a man could look when he bothered to dress himself up.

'Go ahead,' he said. 'I'm listening.'

'This is—this is serious.'

'I'm still listening.' But his eyes were resting on her and his glass was still.

'It's about Patti Jordan. Is she—is she your mistress?' Alexa asked baldly.

His eyelids flickered, but he didn't betray any emotion. He didn't answer for a second or two, then said deliberately, 'Did you ever go to bed with Mark?'

Alexa gasped and colour flooded into her cheeks. 'What kind of a question is that?'

'A very personal one. Just like the one you asked me,' Scott retorted dryly.

'But I had a reason for asking.'

'Other than feminine nosiness, you mean?'

Alexa flushed again but persevered. 'I thought that if she was your mistress, she might be jealous or resent you spending every evening with me, and I just wanted to say that I didn't mind being alone here some nights if you want to be with her. And—and if it helps, I don't mind you telling her the truth about us.'

Scott raised his glass and drank from it, looking at her over the brim, his eyes narrowed. 'That's very noble of you,' he commented. 'Why?'

'Because . . . Well, I saw the way you looked at her and I remembered what you said about loving someone who didn't love you back. And I just thought it might help, that's all.'

'Well, it's certainly a new angle; a bride of only a month encouraging her husband to commit adultery,' Scott observed grimly.

'You can hardly call it committing adultery when we haven't even . . .' Hastily she bit off what she was going to say.

Scott drained his glass and setting it down, got to his feet. 'Haven't even consummated the marriage,' he finished for her. 'As you say.'

He was looking at her rather strangely and Alexa suddenly wondered how much he had had to drink, but she was in no real fear that he wasn't completely in control of himself.

'What gave you the idea that Patti was my mistress?' he demanded suddenly. 'Not just because I danced with her, surely?'

'No. But I saw you talking to her that first day you took me to the Club. You looked—very intimate with her. And then Yvette told me . . .' She hesitated.

'Yes? Just what did Yvette Anderson tell you?' Scott demanded grimly.

'She told me to watch out for Patti. And I took it

that Yvette was trying to warn me that the two of you had been having an affair before you went back to England.' Alexa looked at Scott searchingly. 'Aren't you lovers?'

'No,' he replied shortly. 'And we never have been. Patti is a warm, intelligent woman who has enough sense not to run with the herd. She's good to look at and she's good fun to be with and she doesn't continuously use her femininity as a weapon in her job, which is why she gets on so well with all the men who work with her. And because of that the other women resent her. Especially Yvette.'

'Why especially Yvette?'

'Because her husband, Chris, fell head over heels for Patti last year and was stupid enough to let it show. He was all over Patti for months and she had a hell of a job convincing him that she wasn't interested. In the end she had to get her husband to go round to the Andersons' place and tell him to keep away.' He smiled sardonically. 'I think that's what made Yvette hate Patti most of all: not that her husband had fallen for her, but that Patti didn't find him attractive enough to have an affair with him.'

'Oh, I see. I got it all wrong, then? You're not in love with her?'

'No, I'm not. In the words of the old cliché, Patti and I are just good friends. And I mean that literally.' He looked at her for a moment before adding, 'And for future reference; if I feel like making love to another woman, I shall do just that. And I certainly won't bother to ask your permission first!' He smiled thinly at her startled face and moved towards the door, then paused as if he'd remembered something. 'By the way, *did* you ever sleep with Mark?'

'That's none of your damn business!'

Scott smiled again. 'Goodnight, Alexa.' And left her alone.

It was strange, but from that night Alexa began to feel strangely restless. She still went to the Club most days, but somehow it didn't seem as much fun as it had before. Now she began to notice the undercurrents of gossip and bitchiness among the women which, as she was a newcomer, had been hidden from her previously. A whole load of old scandals would have been poured into her ears if she'd let them. And she found that she was expected to take sides. After the way Scott had danced with Patti at the Club, all the girls in the crowd expected Alexa to share their 'Let's all hate Patti Jordan' viewpoint. But after her talk with Scott she knew that she had no reason to dislike the other girl. Not that she could explain that to the rest of the crowd, of course.

As the days went by Alexa began to look forward more and more to lunchtime when Scott and the other men would join them, especially as Scott started giving her driving lessons after lunch when he said there was less traffic on the roads than at any other time during the day. She was a quick learner and he a good teacher and, possibly because it wasn't his own car, he didn't wince too much when she grated the gears. At first he took her only round the quiet back roads, but as she gained confidence and experience, Scott directed her to take the roads nearer to the town centre where there were lots of Brazilian workers or their dependents always milling about, either on foot or on bicycles, and where the rule of the road among Brazilian drivers tended to be every man for himself. This could be pretty hairy even for fully experienced drivers, and Alexa felt as if she'd lost several pounds in weight when she had emerged from the centre after her first time, her clothes absolutely sticking to her, perspiration trickling down her forehead, and her hands hot and clammy where she had been gripping the wheel so tightly.

'Relax,' Scott advised her. 'You did fine.'

Alexa laughed. 'Thanks, but I think one or two of those cyclists have a few more grey hairs than they started out with! Shall I head for home?'

'Unless you want to go back to the Club?'

'No, I think I'd rather go back to the bungalow.'

She took the long way back, part of the road skirting an area of natural jungle where flowers grew near the edge where there was light. Alexa was always intrigued when passing this spot and would slow the car so that she could get a closer look at the periwinkle plants that grew to five or six feet tall, their blooms large and the same clear blue as her eyes. And there were varieties of violets that grew to the size of shrubs, all of them vying for light and air with the bamboo, which could shoot up by as much as a foot in a single day. But most of all she liked the orchids that seemed to twine themselves round all the other plants and stake their superior claim to the sun.

'Oh, look!' Alexa stopped the car and pointed excitedly. 'There's a monkey!'

Scott leaned across to look. 'It's a capuchin. They usually travel around in groups that can number as many as fifty, but that little fellow looks as if he's lost. Let's go and have a closer look at him, shall we?'

'Oh, yes!'

They got out of the car, leaving the doors open so that they wouldn't frighten it away, and walked slowly across the road. It was a very small monkey, the crest of black hair on top of its otherwise white head resembling the cowl of a monk, which Scott whispered to her was how it got its name. It was the kind of monkey that you sometimes saw with the old-fashioned organ-grinder, dressed in a little red jacket and passing his hat round to collect the pennies. It spotted them as they got near and began to scream and cry out at them angrily, warning them away, but Scott made soothing noises to it and began to unwrap a chocolate bar that he had brought from the car. The monkey stopped screaming and watched, fascinated.

'Here.' Scott broke off a couple of squares of chocolate and gave them to Alexa. 'Hold them out to him and slowly walk nearer. Don't be afraid, he won't hurt you. And they can't resist chocolate.'

Alexa did so, holding her arm out to its fullest extent. The monkey watched her carefully, ready to dash away at the first sudden movement or sign of danger. 'Come on, monkey,' she urged. 'Come and try this nice chocolate.' He rattled off at her again and she thought he was going to go away, but then his greed suddenly overcame his fear and he darted forward, grabbed the chocolate out of her fingers, and ran back again to the safety of his high perch in the trees.

'Look, he likes it.' Alexa laughed delightedly. 'Can I give him some more?'

By the time the chocolate bar was finished the little monkey was eating out of her hand and even allowed her to gently stroke him while he ate.

'Do you want to take him home and keep him as a pet?' Scott asked her.

'Oh, no!' Alexa was horrified at the thought. 'He belongs here in the jungle. I hate seeing animals in cages. I never go to zoos.'

'We'll frighten him off, then, or else he'll follow us to the car.' He clapped his hands loudly and the startled creature bolted up into the trees, railing at them loudly before he ran away.

Alexa watched him go and then stooped to pick some wild orchids before going back to the car. 'Do you remember?' she reminded Scott, 'you said that we might plant some orchids in the garden at the bungalow.'

'So I did. I'll see what I can do.' He spoke lightly enough, but there was a look of intense satisfaction in his eyes that he was careful not to show her.

He was as good as his word and brought home a whole box of plants that same evening.

'I'll get a boy to come tomorrow and plant them for you.'

'Oh, but I'd much rather put them in myself. And they really ought to be done tonight before they start to wilt.' She hesitated. 'Would you mind if I don't go to the Club tonight? You go, of course.'

'Not in the least. I'll stay and help—you could probably use some muscle with the digging.'

After that, Alexa quite often ducked out of going to the Club during the day. She took a keen interest in her orchid plants and routed an old sketchbook and some paints out of her luggage so that she could draw the flowers when they bloomed. She had been quite good at art at school and now spent many absorbed hours trying to get her paintings exactly right, doing one of each variety, looking them up in a book she got out of the library to find their correct names. Often now, too, Scott would take her for a long driving lesson in the evenings, after dinner, and they would spend the rest of the evening at home alone together, reading or listening to music on the radio.

One lunchtime, a week or so after she had begun to learn to drive, Scott picked her up at the Club and took her out for her usual lesson. He seemed rather silent today, but Alexa took little notice as she concentrated on the car.

She passed an open space where, no matter what time of the day, a crowd of dark-haired, dark-eyed little Brazilian boys were always playing football, many of them barefoot, their one burning ambition to be another Pele. As she drove, the sky clouded over and it began to rain. By now Alexa was used to the sudden downpours, but they were so heavy that it was almost impossible for the windscreen wipers to keep up, so she pulled off the road on to the uneven verge under some trees. The staccato drumming of rain on the metal roof of the car was blunted a little by the branches and they could at least hear themselves speak. Alexa switched off the engine and leaned back in her seat, waiting for it to stop.

Scott unbuttoned the pocket of his shirt, took out a blue airmail envelope and dropped it in her lap. 'This came for you this morning.'

He went on to light a cigarette while Alexa gazed down at the envelope without picking it up. She recognized Elaine's writing straightaway; they had exchanged so many letters over the years, had always kept in close touch—until now. It was a very fat envelope, just bursting to be opened so that all the news could come pouring out. It would be full of words like honeymoon, happy, new house, wonderful—and the name Mark would be there over and over and over again.

'You don't have to read it.' Scott's voice broke harshly into her thoughts. 'You can just open the window and throw it out into the trees. It will soon rot down into nothing in this climate.'

Just like all living things, Alexa thought irrelevantly.

They all rot down to nothing in the end. Flowers, trees, animals, people. No matter how beautiful the flower, or how tall and strong the tree, how fast and graceful the animal, or how sad or happy the people, in the end it was all one. Slowly she put her thumb under the flap of the envelope and tore it open. She sensed rather than heard Scott draw in his breath sharply, but she didn't turn to look at him as she began to read.

She had been right; Mark's name appeared in almost every other line, but Alexa's expression didn't change as she carefully read through the pages, turning them one by one. Towards the end Elaine had written: 'I expect you think that this letter is one long gush, but oh, Alexa, I can't begin to tell you how happy I am. Your being hurt was the only blot on the landscape, if you know what I mean. But now that you've fallen in love with Scott and married him everything is really perfect. And Mark is such a wonderful lover; he makes me feel like a fat, contented cat purring in the sun. I'm sure that if Scott is anywhere near as good, then you, too, must be wonderfully happy. Aren't we lucky to have each found the man we love—and in such a strange way?'

Alexa finished the letter, put the pages neatly back in order and then passed it to Scott to read, her features still quite expressionless. He glanced at her and then bent his head, reading more quickly than she had done. Wryly she wondered what he would make of that last paragraph.

At length he finished and turned towards her. 'So Mark has turned out to be the ideal husband. Just as you knew he would. And the ideal lover in bed,' he added caustically when she didn't answer. 'Doesn't that make you jealous, Alexa? Picturing the two of them in bed together? Especially if you slept with him yourself and know what he was like.' He waited for her to turn and let fly at him, to shout at him to shut up, but she remained motionless, gazing straight ahead through the windscreen at the pelting rain. Angrily he reached out and caught her by the shoulders, making her turn to look at him. 'Was he good in bed, Alexa? Was he?' he demanded, his fingers biting into her flesh.

She stared into his eyes for a long moment, then said quite steadily, 'Why are you trying to goad me into losing my temper?'

Scott's eyes widened in surprise, then he let go of her and sat back. 'Don't you know?'

'Yes, I think so. You're afraid that Elaine's letter will make me get depressed again, so you're trying to make me angry instead.'

'And are you—depressed by it?'

Shaking her head slowly, Alexa answered, 'No. It's strange, I thought I would be, but I just feel . . .' she shrugged, 'sort of sad, I suppose.'

'Sad? For yourself?'

She wrinkled her forehead. 'Not really. It's the sort of feeling you get when you go to see a terribly sad film. Your heart gets wrung like mad, but you know that it's hopeless and there's nothing you can do about it. You come out feeling battered and bruised, but then it just fades away and becomes a memory.'

While she had been speaking, Scott had had his eyes fixed on her face and now he gave a soft sigh. 'You know, Alexa, I think you just started to get over Mark.'

'No!' The denial was instantaneous. 'I shall never get over Mark. And I don't want to. He will always have the first place in my heart.'

Scott's face darkened and for an instant his eyes flamed with anger, but was quickly masked. 'Let's get going, shall we?' he said shortly. 'The rain's stopped and I'm due back at work.'

CHAPTER SIX

'*Bom dia*, Maria. Er—*ovos mexidos por pegueno almoco, por favor.*'

The maid laughed but looked pleased at Alexa's stumbling attempt to ask for scrambled eggs for her breakfast. She had found a Portuguese phrasebook among the books from Scott's apartment and every day she tried to add a few words to her vocabulary, much to Maria's amusement. Now the girl made her go over it a couple of times more to get the pronunciation right.

While she cooked the eggs, Alexa wandered out into the garden to look at her orchids; she was waiting for one particular plant to come into full bloom so that she could paint it. Today was Saturday, and Scott had gone into the office, but would be home early and had promised to bring a car of her own for her. It would be nice to have her own set of wheels and not have to rely on Scott or Yvette to provide transport. Not that she saw too much of Yvette now; that friendship had cooled when Alexa made it plain that she wasn't interested in listening to gossip or taking sides. When she went to the Club now she mingled with all the wives, not confining herself to just one set alone. And she had made a point of speaking to Patti Jordan whenever she saw the other girl there, which had further alienated Yvette.

But strangely Alexa had found that not being tied to the crowd, instead of making her feel lonely, had given her a kind of freedom and she could enjoy the Club for what it offered instead of making it the hub of her existence. She was grateful to Yvette for her friendship because she realised that she had needed those few weeks of cocooned existence to recover from the traumatic times that had gone before. She had needed to lose herself in new places, new people, new interests, before she could start to be herself and rely on herself again. But now she felt better, better than she had done since Mark rejected her, and ready to start living again.

After breakfast she pulled a lounger with a fat, soft mattress out into the sun and lay on it in her bikini, adding another shade to an already attractive golden tan. She must have slept, because she didn't hear Scott come home and was only aware of him when she woke and found him standing over her. As she opened her eyes, she looked straight up at him and surprised a strange look on his face as his eyes ran over her body, a bleak, almost haunted look, mixed with a kind of yearning. His grey eyes came up to her face, saw that she was awake, and the expression was immediately gone so that she wasn't sure that she'd even seen it.

'Well, sleepyhead, don't you want to see your car?' Scott demanded, his voice quite normal.

'Is it here?' Alexa jumped up and groped for her sandals. 'Can we go out in it now?'

'Sure. But I think you'd better change into something more than three triangles of material, unless you want to cause a traffic jam in town,' he told her flippantly.

Alexa laughed. 'The other motorists are all too busy playing dodgem cars to look at me! Give me two minutes,' she called to him over her shoulder as she ran to the house, her dark hair swirling round her head, her body long-limbed and graceful. Scott watched her go, then took out a cigarette and lit it with hands that were strangely unsteady.

The car was an American one, as were most of those in Jari, and bigger than most English cars. It took a little getting used to after Scott's much heavier and shorter car and Alexa was glad that he was sitting beside her on her first time out.

'Let's make a day of it, shall we?' he suggested. 'All you've really seen yet is the town. We could drive out to the nurseries and take a look at how we grow the tree seedlings first, if you're interested.'

'Fine.' Alexa was in the mood to be pleased to do anything today.

They headed out of town towards the airport a few miles from Monte Dourado, to Plan Alto, a village built where the jungle had been cleared several years ago. Scott directed her to drive down a dirt road to the left and they pulled up about half a mile further on and got out of the car. They were in a large cleared area of several hundred acres with row upon row of tree seedlings of various heights stretching almost as far as the eye could see.

Alexa looked around her, awed by the immensity of the undertaking. 'These are all gmelina seedlings?'

'That's right. We also grow pines, but that nursery is some miles away. It mostly works out that there are more pines in the south where the soil is sandy, and the gmelinas in the north. Our goal is a balance of both softwood and hardwood to supply the whole range of timber products.' He stopped and grinned. 'Sorry, I was starting to lecture, wasn't I?'

'I don't mind. Tell me some more. Why this particular tree?'

So, as they drove on through the vast plantations of growing timber, Scott explained how the project came into being and the experiments that had taken place before the foresters had found the ideal tree for the climate and conditions, one strangely enough that was native to Burma and India and had never been grown in the Amazon basin before. He spoke eloquently, evidently enthusiastic about the subject and making her realise just how much of an exciting venture it was to try and tame such a primitive land.

The plantations went on for miles, mostly gmelina but here and there strands of pine which acted as firebreaks and which had been fenced in so that fat white cattle could graze on the grass that had been specially sown for them among the young trees. They were heading south-east now, towards the River Jari itself. Once, in the distance, they saw a fast diesel train overtaking them, its seemingly endless trail of wagons loaded with huge tree trunks which Scott told her were headed for Munguba where the sawmill and pulp mill were awaiting them.

Munguba was where they were heading themselves. This, too, was a new town, purpose-built on the banks of the river to house the staff needed to man all the new mills and to work the surrounding rice and vegetable fields.

'Why do they need so much rice?' Alexa wanted to know.

Scott grinned. 'It's one of the staple foods here. Haven't you noticed how many rice dishes Maria gives us?'

'Yes, and she would probably give us more if I hadn't protested. Rice isn't at all good for the figure.'

As if that was an invitation, Scott let his eyes wander slowly over her. 'You'll do,' he said softly. 'Believe me, you'll do.'

Alexa laughed uncertainly, not sure how to take it.

She was going to make some remark about playing so much tennis, but her voice dried in her throat and she concentrated on finding somewhere to park. They ate in a small restaurant with gaily checked tablecloths and Scott ordered the Brazilian national dish called *feijoada* which everyone seemed to eat every Saturday lunchtime. It consisted mostly of several different kinds of meat, black beans, tomatoes and tabasco peppers to make it hot, served over rice and with lots of side dishes. They finished with fruit; there was always lots of huge, succulent fruit available at any time of the year in Brazil.

Afterwards they strolled around the town for a little, but then Scott took over the car and drove her out to the huge pulp mill on the edge of the river. To Alexa it was just a huge and very modern factory which she was quite willing to believe could process seven hundred and fifty tons of timber in a day. Scott took her round it and she was impressed by its size and computerized efficiency, but then he told her that the whole thing had been towed half-way across the world from Japan, ready built, on two immense floating platforms, and she stared at him in genuine amazement.

'You mean they really towed something that big?'

'That's right. All two hundred million dollars' worth of it.'

'Wow!' Alexa looked at the mill with new respect. 'But it looks so—so permanent. How did they get it on to the land?'

Scott started to explain it to her, taking a notebook from his pocket and drawing a simple diagram for her. Alexa leaned nearer to see, their heads close together. She caught a trace of the woody, masculine after-shave he used and her mind wandered. His thick, dark hair had a slight curl in it where it grew in the nape of his neck, and he had a very small scar just below his left ear, near the hairline, that she had never noticed before.

'Do you get it so far?' Scott turned suddenly and caught her watching him. For a moment their eyes met and held, Alexa felt an odd sort of tightening in her chest and turned away in some confusion, while Scott's eyes grew thoughtful.

'Yes, I understand. They put in some pilings, then built a dam between the river and the platforms so that it flooded the pilings, floated the platforms into position and then pumped the water out again. And, hey presto, you have a mill all ready to start work. Neat.'

Her voice sounded rushed and over-bright even to her own ears, but at least it had covered that slight breathlessness in her chest.

'Tell you what.' Scott put away his notebook and glanced at his watch. 'Why don't we go back to Monte Dourado by river instead of driving back?'

'It sounds fine. But what about the car?'

'That can come too. Let's drive down to the wharf and I'll see if I can fix it.'

He fixed it so well that within half an hour a passing ferry boat belonging to the company, on its way to Monte Dourado, loaded down with passengers and cargo, pulled into the wharf and they and the car were quickly taken aboard. The captain himself greeted them and took them up to the bridge for the first few miles of the trip. They stood together on the outside starboard wing of the bridge where a slight breeze lifted the humidity and made the heat pleasantly bearable. Whereas the road from Monte Dourado to Munguba went straight across country, the river

meandered round a big curve that doubled the
distance. Mostly the banks on either side were thick
with trees and undergrowth that grew right down to
the water's edge, but here and there the trees had been
cleared and there was a cluster of small, thatched
houses built up high on stilts, perched on the river
bank.

'Why are they up on stilts?' Alexa demanded.

'Because the heavy rainfall and the melting snow
from the Andes make the river rise during the rainy
season. Sometimes it comes up as much as seven or
eight feet. If they didn't build the houses on stilts they
would all be swept away every year. But it's quite mild
here, really. In Manaos, way back inland on the
Amazon itself, the water can rise as much as *sixty* feet.
There whole villages have to float their homes on rafts
or pontoons until the water goes down again.'

There were lots of boats on the river, ranging from
large cargo boats like their own flying the colourful
green, gold and blue flag of Brazil, right down to small
motor boats and home-made dug-out canoes. Alexa
watched, fascinated, as they passed one dug-out,
rowed by a man kneeling at each end, so loaded down
with barrels and bales that there was hardly any of the
boat showing above the waterline.

'Oh, dear, I do hope they don't tip over,' she
remarked as the ferryboat's wash made the crude craft
wobble precariously.

'Not half as much as they do,' Scott returned
grimly. He pointed to the other bank, putting his
other hand on her shoulder. 'Look over there. See
them? Half a dozen alligators just waiting to grab any
poor devil that's unlucky enough to fall in.'

For a moment Alexa couldn't make them out, but
then one of them moved and she saw the long green

shapes like giant lizards lying in the sun on the bank of red mud. Instinctively she recoiled, moving closer to Scott. His hand tightened on her shoulder and she stiffened, then slowly relaxed but didn't move away. He pointed out other things to her, like the jaburu storks, some six feet high, and flamingoes wading daintily along the shores, their feathers an unbelievably beautiful pink. There were white butterflies as big as saucers fluttering above the foliage, the leaves of which glistened so brightly in the sun that Alexa imagined that they had been stamped out of pieces of shining gold.

Alexa loved it all, drinking in all the new sights, and it was quite some time before they went down below to get a drink. And it was only then that Scott took his hand from her shoulder.

The day was almost done as the boat rounded the last bend in the river before Monte Dourado and the captain blew his horn to let them know they were coming in to land. Alexa looked expectantly towards the left bank to see the town, but was astonished to see just as many buildings on the other side.

'What's that place?' she asked, pointing.

'I suppose you could call it the other half of Monte Dourado. It's a township that has built up and lives like a parasite off the new town. Once the town began to be established, outsiders from all over the eastern Amazon basin started coming here on the river and settled across the Rio Jari, outside the company-owned land.'

'Why did they come here? To get work?'

'No, although some of the families of the men who work here do stay there until they can get permanent housing in the new town. Mostly they come to trade or to provide services for the thousands of people who are working here. Now there are probably more people living there than in Monte Dourado, and they have their own mayor and police force.'

Alexa could well believe it, for the buildings lined the river bank for over a mile, built entirely on rough wooden pilings driven into the mud right on the edge of the water. There seemed to be no design to the place, the wooden buildings were of all shapes and sizes and reminded Alexa of a shanty town in the gold rush days. There was a great deal of noise and traffic, with motor launches tied up alongside unloading goods, young boys skilfully manoeuvring small canoes and lots of shiny aluminium boats with noisy outboard motors darting backwards and forwards across the river, all of them somehow managing to avoid each other.

'Good heavens, it's like Piccadilly Circus in the rush hour!' Alexa exclaimed as she watched a small boat disappear almost under their bows and then miraculously reappear on the other side to angry blasts of the horn.

'Worse, I should think.' Scott nodded towards the other bank. 'How would you like to go over there some time?'

'I'd love it. Why haven't we been there before? I hadn't even heard of it.'

He shrugged. 'The Club types don't go over there much,' he told her disparagingly. 'At least not the women. It's too earthy for them. They prefer the cushioned luxury and exclusiveness of the new town.'

'What about the men?'

His mouth curved in amusement. 'Oh, some of them go over there—quite often,' he added with a grin, as if at some inner joke.

'When can we go?'

'Tomorrow, if you like. I think it's some sort of feast day.' He straightened up from where he had been leaning on the rail. 'I think they're about ready for us to drive the car off now.'

They had dinner at a restaurant in the town and Alexa went to bed almost as soon as they got home, tired and looking forward to tomorrow. It was only as she leaned forward to turn off the bedside lamp that she caught sight of Mark's photograph and realised that she hadn't thought about him once all day.

After breakfast the next morning, Alexa drove them down to the wharf where they left the car and stood in line to wait for a river taxi to take them across. This turned out to be one of the shiny boats that she had seen yesterday endlessly ferrying people across the river. They didn't have to wait very long, and took their places among a crowd of gaily dressed men, women and children who were all talking non-stop at the tops of their voices.

On the other side, Scott helped her out of the boat and they climbed a wooden staircase up into the town. To Alexa's surprise she found that the main street was made up of wooden planking that separated long rows of houses and shops on either side. Some of the houses were quite large, two-storeyed places, and further along there was a department store and a big food market.

'Here, you might need this.' Scott gave her some money which she slipped into her bag. 'But don't forget that you're supposed to haggle over everything you buy.'

Already there was a carnival atmosphere in the air. Somewhere a samba band was playing and the music seemed to have infected the people who were singing and laughing as they walked along the street, some of them even swaying and clapping to the music. The sun was starting to get hot and all the cafés had their awnings up or sunshades over the tables out in the open. It was colourful, gay, noisy and busy, and Alexa loved it.

She turned a laughing face to Scott. 'They all seem terrifically happy. It must be a very special day.'

'Not really. It's just an excuse for a party. Let's walk up towards the band.'

It became more crowded as they walked on, but Alexa didn't mind in the least. She was busy watching the women haggling over a purchase or gazing at the vast displays of fruit in the market: bananas, shiny oranges, pineapples, huge melons, mangoes, guavas, passionfruit—the list seemed to be endless, and then there were stalls with flowers, vegetables, groceries, and one with the most strange and odd-looking fish she had ever seen; nothing at all like the local fishmonger's slabs back home.

They stopped at a stall where Scott bought her a bracelet with a good luck charm on it in the shape of a clenched fist with the thumb sticking up between the first and second fingers. 'You must have one of these,' he told her. 'It wards off evil.'

'Oh, Maria has one. She wears it all the time.' Alexa smiled at him. 'I didn't realise you were superstitious. Does it really work?'

'Only if someone gives it to you as a gift—it's no good if you buy it for yourself.' He fastened it on her wrist. 'There, now you should be safe from any evil spirits.'

Alexa laughed. 'Now I must buy you something.' Looking around, she saw a man selling lottery tickets and darted across to him. In her best Portuguese she asked for the ticket of her choice and the seller took

her money and handed over the change. Turning back
to Scott, she presented him with the ticket with mock
gravity, saying, 'You must keep this very carefully,
because the man assures me that it will most definitely
win the first prize of half a million *cruzeiros*.'

He grinned. 'I bet he says that to all the beautiful
girls!'

As he took the ticket from her their hands touched
and Alexa found herself gazing into his eyes, eyes that
had grown suddenly intense. Someone jostled her and
she stumbled against his chest. His hands came up to
steady her and stayed on her bare arms.

'Oh. Sorry,' she muttered, that queer, breathless
feeling in her chest again. For a long moment he
continued to hold her, then she looked away with a
shaky laugh. 'It's getting really crowded. And hot. Do
you think we could have a drink?'

'Yes, of course.' Scott guided her to the nearest café
and they sat down under an orange, green and yellow
sunshade. He ordered *cafezinho*, which turned out to
be black, very sweet and very strong coffee, served in
small cups which were burning hot to the touch.

Alexa sipped her coffee slowly, content to sit and
watch the passing parade: the families in their best
clothes, the children especially beautifully dressed,
and the young girls walking always with a companion,
their eyes constantly on the look-out for young men
and lowered demurely whenever any came in sight.
And the young men, how they strutted like flamboyant
roosters, hand on hip, swaying exaggeratedly to the
music, openly eyeing all the girls, some of them
carrying radios that added to the general din.

'Why do they go around like that? Are they trying to
pick the girls up?'

'Probably not. They're only trying to impress them.'

'I wouldn't be very impressed by it.'

'That's because you're English. Brazilian men take their masculinity very seriously and appearances have to be maintained at all costs. It's not enough to be male, other people have to be made aware of your virility. And they are extremely possessive in their attitudes to their wives and girl-friends.'

And not only Brazilians, Alexa thought wryly; she'd known several Englishmen who had exactly the same attitude, although considering themselves quite free to do as they liked, of course. At a table nearby some men began to argue and soon became heated, getting to their feet and throwing their arms about as they emphasised the point they were trying to make. Alexa looked at them in some alarm, expecting a fight to break out at any second, but Scott and everyone else seemed quite unperturbed and, in fact, within minutes the men had quietened down and were laughing together again.

'Phew! Do they often get that excited?' she asked.

'Most of the time, but their arguments aren't usually bad-tempered. 'They're a very easy-going people as a whole.'

'They seem to be a very mixed race,' Alexa observed as she looked at the faces going past and saw every colour from white through to almost black.

'They are, more so than most places in the world except perhaps the United States. The Portuguese who first settled here inter-bred with the native Indians and Negro slaves brought over from Africa. Then there were waves of immigrants from Europe, the Middle East and Japan who were all absorbed into the community. But, unlike the States, discrimination based on race or colour is virtually unknown here. And they don't have bloody revolutions like other

South American countries. In Brazil passions only rise when people start discussing the merits of their favourite football teams.'

Alexa laughed and would have asked him some more, but the sound of the band was coming closer and it was difficult to hear.

'The procession's coming; we'd better get to the front if you want to watch it.'

They moved out into the sun again and stood among the crowds of people who were forming at either side of the street. Alexa put on her dark glasses, but she could feel the heat beating down on to her bare head and shoulders. 'You need a hat,' Scott told her. 'Stay here and I'll get you one.'

He stepped back into the crowd and Alexa craned forward to see if the procession was in view, but there was no sign of it yet. Two little boys slipped in front of her, giggling and sucking sweets. On her right an ample-bosomed matron in a red and white dress clapped her hands to the music. She felt someone move in beside her on her left and a hand touched her arm. Thinking it was Scott, Alexa turned and found herself smiling up at a complete stranger, a young olive-skinned man with long hair and a shirt open to the waist of his tight-fitting jeans. He smiled at her and said something she didn't understand, his hand stroking her bare arm. Alexa tried to edge away, but was hemmed in by the people around her and looked round hopefully for Scott.

He was working his way through the crowd towards her, but must have seen the appeal in her eyes, because the next second he was at her side. For a moment the two men faced each other out, then the young Brazilian realised what he was up against and melted away to look for easier game. Alexa watched him go, thinking that it proved her point; Scott had been just as possessive as any Brazilian, even over someone he didn't love. But then, of course, she did bear his name, which in a man's eyes probably amounted to the same thing. Alexa put on the straw hat he had bought her, glad of its protection from the sun and also because it hid her face from him a little.

The procession, headed by a samba band wearing exotic pink costumes, came into view, the players dancing to their own music as they travelled along. Behind them came women, again dressed in pink, with gold turbans or else immense Carmen Miranda-type hats on their heads. More dancers and bands followed, all in costumes as colourful and beautiful as the wearer could afford, the children in smaller versions of their parents' costumes. The noise was immense, everyone singing, beating drums or letting off fire-crackers. Scott tried to say something to her, but Alexa couldn't hear and laughingly shook her head. He tried again, putting an arm across her shoulders to pull her nearer, his mouth close to her ear. 'We should have remembered to bring a camera with us.'

She nodded, looking into his eyes and quickly away, feeling the weight of his arm across her shoulders, the warmth of his skin against her own, until after a couple of minutes, he removed it.

It took the procession a long time to pass for the simple reason that members of the crowd kept joining on to the tail like an endless crocodile.

After an hour or so of it, Scott jerked his thumb backwards out of the crowd and she nodded, glad to get out of the sun and the crowd of hot, sweaty people. He took her to a restaurant where they had long cold drinks followed by a leisurely lunch. It was cool in here, a central fan turning to circulate the air. When they had eaten they sat over their coffee, listening to the sound of the music outside. The charm on her new bracelet jingled as it hit the side of her cup.

'Are the people here really that superstitious? They don't believe in the evil eye nowadays, surely?'

'A great many of them do. Especially older people who live in the country and haven't had any education. Ghosts, witches and strange beasts are believed in all over the country and a good trade goes on for spells for anything from a good harvest to keeping your husband or wife faithful.'

'You're kidding!' Alexa protested. 'I don't believe it.'

'It's true enough. Remember it's only in the last generation or so that all children have gone to school. Most schools work on a shift system because there aren't enough places to go round. In Monte Dourado there are a thousand children who go to school during the day and eight hundred illiterate adults who study at night.'

'So they really believe in ghosts and spells and things?'

'Of course. The Indians especially. They believe in a thing called the Capelobo, who has an ant-eater's head on a human body and who stalks the jungle looking for lone travellers to kill.'

'Ugh! Gruesome! I'm glad I'm not likely to meet him.'

Scott grinned. 'And there was I going to ask you if you'd like to take the trip with me next time I have to go to one of our advance clearing camps.'

'Out into the jungle?'

'On the edge of it where we've established a camp to house the labourers who're working there. We'd go part way by train and then by helicopter. It's quite an impressive sight, seeing the Rio Jari and the work we've already done on the project from the air.'

'When are you going?' Alexa asked, playing for time while she made up her mind.

'In a couple of weeks or so, I expect.' Scott was watching her keenly. 'Well, will you come?'

'How long will it be for?'

His mouth thinned into the sardonic smile she hadn't seen for some time. 'You don't have to worry; we can go there and back in a day.'

'All right, I'd like to go.'

'Not afraid of the Capelobo?' he asked, not meaning that at all.

'No. Should I be?'

'Not at all.' He stood up to leave, his tone mocking. 'You'll be quite safe as long as you're with me.'

They stayed in the town for the rest of the day, wandering round the shops and watching the procession again as it wound along the street for the second time, but in the dark now with everyone carrying torches and lanterns. If anything it was noisier and people let their hair down more as they danced, grabbing hold of spectators in the crowds and pulling them into the procession. Some were drinking as they went and it was obvious that things were getting a bit out of hand.

'Time for us to go, I think.' Scott led her towards the steps where the taxis moored.

They moved on down the street and came to a two-storeyed building with a veranda that was brightly lit with garishly coloured light-bulbs strung along its length. Outside and on the veranda young girls were standing, all of them heavily made up and wearing low-cut dresses or tight skirts and figure-hugging tops. Some men, better dressed than most of the others, were passing in the other direction and the girls called out to them, beckoning them over. After a few words and some laughter, the men each paired up with a girl and went inside. Alexa realised at once that the place must be a brothel, and it became clear to her why Scott had said earlier that the men from Monte Dourado came over here a whole lot more than the women did. Obviously this was just another of the 'services' that the shanty town provided.

They sat in the boat taking them across the river and Alexa looked back at the wooden town, seeing the bright lights of the procession creating a sort of halo of light above the darker outline of the buildings, but she wasn't thinking about the town at all. She was intensely aware of Scott squashed close to her side in the small crowded boat, his arm around her shoulders again. She had found, during that one night when they had almost made love, that he was highly sexed and very experienced, and now she couldn't help wondering if he, too, had ever made use of the services provided by the girls she had seen.

During the following week, Alexa enjoyed the freedom that having her own car gave her. She drove herself to the Club for her morning game of tennis, glad that she didn't have to rely on Yvette any more, and afterwards either drove home or explored the town alone, before meeting Scott for lunch, either at the Club again or at one of the Brazilian restaurants in the town where they tried more exotic dishes. Her trip to the shanty town across the river had aroused an interest in Brazil, and in the afternoons she dug out some of Scott's books on the subject and would read for an hour or so when she wasn't painting.

At the weekend Scott said he had a surprise for her and took her down to the wharf where they went

aboard a small motor launch carrying supplies for
some of the villages further upriver. The boat went
slowly compared to the big ferry boat and Alexa found
it rather unnerving at first to be so close to the water,
especially when she saw the alligators on the banks,
but everyone else seemed to be quite nonchalant about
it and she gradually lost her fear. At every village they
came to people would row out in dug-out canoes
loaded down with fruit or vegetables to trade. In the
main river they passed other boats carrying brazil nuts
or rubber tapped from the trees on their way
downstream, but soon the launch turned into a smaller
tributary where the way was much narrower and the
jungle overhung the water. Exotically coloured birds
flew among the branches; Scott pointed out big
macaws with their hooked beaks and long tails and the
smaller red and green parrots and parakeets which
kept up a noisy clamour in the treetops. He identified
hornbills and vultures, and made her listen to the
clear, flutelike notes of the irapurus and the mournful
sound of the bellbird that sounded exactly like the
tolling of a funeral bell.

They caught sight of animals coming down to the
water's edge to drink: wild pigs and once a fully-
grown tapir that looked like something straight out of
the stone age. But everywhere there were monkeys, of
all sizes and colours, swinging through the trees,
jabbering nineteen to the dozen, hanging by their tails
while they stuffed bananas into their greedy mouths.

'Oh, look at that one!' Alexa leaned over the rail and
pointed excitedly to where a spider monkey leapt
across a gap in the trees that must have been at least
thirty feet across.

'Fantastic, aren't they?' Scott reached over and
pulled her arm back in. 'Better not to lean out when

that johnny's about,' he explained, nodding towards the water.

Alexa looked down and nearly died. Swimming along beside the boat, its body humped and glistening, swam a huge snake, its ugly head with its loose-hinged jaws moving along just a few inches above the surface. Immediately she moved backwards with a cry of horror. 'Oh, God! What is it? It's huge.'

'It's an anaconda. Probably about thirty feet long, I should think. They're pretty mean-tempered hunters and often attack for no reason, so it's best not to get too close.'

Alexa crossed her arms over her chest, hugging her shoulders. 'Lord, I hate snakes!'

Scott led her further into the boat. 'Here, sit down and have a drink. Sorry if it spoilt things for you, but it's best to warn you.'

He sat her down on a wooden crate and went to get a couple of cold drinks from the fridge in the cabin, coming back to share her box. 'You're shivering.' He began to rub her bare arms until the goosebumps went down. 'Okay now?'

'Yes, thanks.' But she kept close to his side for the rest of the trip, not venturing too near the rail again and not objecting at all when he put a comforting arm round her waist and kept it there most of the day. And that night, when she was alone in her bedroom, Alexa picked up the photograph of Mark, stood looking at it for a long time and then carefully packed it away in one of the drawers of her dressing table, face down.

When Scott came home from work about ten days later, he told her that he had to go out to one of the forestry camps on the following Wednesday and there was room for her in the helicopter if she still wanted to go. Alexa hesitated, remembering the anaconda, but there was a distinct challenge in Scott's grey eyes that made her lift her chin and say, 'Yes, of course I still want to go.'

'Good girl!' His eyes grew warm and he reached out to touch her hand. 'I'll make all the arrangements, then. We'll have to leave pretty early in the morning.'

'What shall I wear?'

He laughed. 'That's always the first thing a woman thinks about!'

'Well, I'm sorry, but . . .'

Scott stood up and put a finger against her lips. 'Don't be sorry. I like feminine women.' Gently he moved his finger, slowly tracing the outline of her mouth. Alexa stood quite still, gazing up into his face, seeing his eyes darken. He moved his hand to cup her chin and his other hand clasped her arm. 'Alexa.' His voice sounded strangely hoarse as he said her name.

'*Senhora*, the dinner, she is ready. You come?' Maria's cheerful voice called to them from the dining-room.

For a moment Scott's grip tightened, then a rueful look came into his eyes and he stepped away. 'You'd better wear jeans and a pair of walking shoes. Oh, and take a sweater or jacket in case it gets chilly coming back on the train.'

He didn't attempt to touch her again, but Alexa was very aware of him all evening, and especially when they said goodnight and went to their separate rooms.

On Wednesday they got up very early and caught the first train travelling north. There were a couple of other technicians that Alexa already knew, as well as about twenty forestry workers with them in the one passenger carriage of the train, but behind it stretched a long tail of empty goods wagons going back to be loaded up with timber to take down to Munguba to fuel the boilers at the pulp mill. At the end of the line they got off and, with the two technicians, walked across to the helicopter that was waiting nearby, Scott humping a box of the supplies that he had bought back in England which he told her he intended to hand out to the local Indians.

The flight in the helicopter was as stupendous as Scott had promised it would be. The forestry plantations stretched for mile upon mile in bands of light green pine and darker gmelina, with in the distance the deep, dark green vegetation of the virgin forest. Long, thin straight lines of roads bisected the plantations at every few miles, but there was no sign of life until the pilot went a few miles out of his way and showed them a wide trail being blazed through the jungle towards the West.

'It's the Transamazonica,' Scott told her. 'The new road that's being built to link up with Peru and Columbia. They hope eventually to link up from Brazil to Canada via the Pan American highway.'

The new road was impressive, but Alexa preferred it when they flew up the course of the Rio Jari and she saw the wide San Antonio falls which stretched all the way across the river, the water gushing down the steep rocks in foaming, crashing torrents. One of the technicians started telling her how they hoped to harness its power for hydro-electricity to supply Monte Dourado, but Alexa wasn't really listening, she was far too fascinated watching the falls, and quite honestly wished he would be quiet; these technicians never seemed to be able to let nature alone.

The helicopter landed in a clearing near a temporary forestry camp comprised entirely of wooden huts with corrugated iron roofs. The technicians went off to take soil samples while Scott spoke to the man in charge of the tree clearing. They talked for some time and then Scott took her with him into the edge of the jungle, showing her where they had first cut out all the good trees that were free from defects or pests and would make building timber, and then the secondary trees to be used as boiler fuel. The rest of the vegetation would be burnt as soon as they had three days in a row when it didn't rain and the stuff was dry enough to burn.

They had lunch sitting out in the open at a long table, all the workers together. The meal was cooked and served from an open-air kitchen, and Alexa wisely didn't ask what they were eating. It tasted okay, though, and it was fun to sit beside Scott and try to understand what the workers were laughing and joking about, especially when they looked at her and made some remarks that made Scott laugh.

'What did they say?' she demanded.

'I'd better not tell you, you'll only get bigheaded.'

'No, really? Please tell me.'

'Well, in essence, it was that I must be a very lucky and satisfied man.'

'Oh!' Alexa coloured and the men all laughed delightedly.

When they had eaten he let her go into the jungle to look for new species of orchids while he got on with his task of working out which and how many seedlings would be needed to plant in the cleared ground. 'Keep near the edge,' he warned her. 'Don't go too far.' Not that Alexa had the slightest intention of going far in; she was much too scared of any snakes that might be lurking in the trees or undergrowth for that.

The orchids only grew where there was light, so she found several new varieties quite near the cleared area, although there were many that she had already painted. She went along the track made by the tractors, seeing the stumps of trees which hadn't yet been burnt. A butterfly, its iridescent, metallic blue wings shimmering in the shadows, flew close by, its irregular flight like a happy, carefree dance. Alexa exclaimed with delight and followed it to a small forest pool where it joined what looked like a hundred more of the same kind. She watched them with great pleasure for a while and then caught sight of a pair of humming-birds, their wings like jewels, hovering over a particularly beautiful orchid which had rooted itself in the hollow of a branch and hung down, weaving among the woody vines of a liana. Using a stick, she triumphantly hooked down the flower and added it to the growing collection in her hand. It was quite light here, the sun shining down through the cleared trees, not like she had expected the jungle to be at all. And she was quite safe, she could hear the sound of a tractor in the distance and still see tree stumps poking through the undergrowth.

A spider monkey jabbered at her from a tree and threw a brazil nut at her. Alexa laughed and picked up the nut to throw it back. Immediately he caught it and shied it at her again, moving on a few yards. Alexa laughingly joined in the game, following him along until he threw the nut down into thick undergrowth where she couldn't find it.

'Sorry, chum, you'll have to find some other dog to fetch your stick.' She turned to go back and realised that she had wandered away from the trail of tractor marks. But there was the stump of a tree about thirty yards away, so it must be somewhere near. But the stump turned out to be a jagged natural one, not sawn at all, and she began to get worried. Forcing herself to keep calm, she stood quite still and listened for the sound of the tractor. Faintly she heard what sounded

like it, but the noise came from a deeper, thicker part
of the jungle. Alexa looked doubtfully in the direction,
but then thought that perhaps the men were clearing
that part of the forest and if she walked towards it she
would soon come upon them. She set off confidently
enough, but was soon having to push her way through
quite dense foliage, and when she stood still ten
minutes later, the sound had gone completely and she
knew that she was lost.

Immediately she panicked and tried to go back the
way she had come, yelling for help at the top of her
voice. She ran on, pushing the branches out of the way
with her arms, her breath coming in terrified sobs.
Twigs and undergrowth caught at her hair and
clothes, but she ran on, dropping her bunch of orchids
and leaving them scattered in her wake. Only when she
had no breath left did she come to a stop and lean, her
chest heaving, against a tree, tears running down her
face, more afraid than she had ever been in her life.

Afraid to move but even more afraid to stay still,
Alexa pushed on through the jungle, trying to find her
way back. The soil beneath her feet felt damp now and
the vegetation was so thick that she could hardly see
the sun. Once she stopped to rest and felt something
on her bare arm, and looked down to see a huge spider
with black furry legs crawling on her skin. With a cry
of horror, she shook it off and jerked away, again
trying to push her way out of the jungle. She wasn't
sure quite when she found the path; one moment she
was pushing her way through the trees, the next they
seemed to clear a little and the undergrowth wasn't so
dense. Thankfully Alexa began to follow it, hoping
desperately that it would lead her to the camp. It was
terribly hot and humid down there among the thick
trunks of the trees; Alexa paused to wipe the

perspiration out of her eyes, leaving a black streak across her face. Her breath rasped in her throat and she longed for a drink. As she pushed on it grew even hotter and what little light there was disappeared as the sky took on a yellow tinge and grew darker. The birds and animals fell silent and there was a strange feeling of danger in the air.

Alexa stopped again, the only noise the sound of her own gasping breath. She whimpered with fear, looking all around her, not knowing where the danger was coming from, the story of the Capelobo who killed lone travellers filling her mind with dread. But then she heard the distant rumble of thunder and immediately a great wind came roaring through the forest, bending even the great crowns of the trees. Monkeys scurried past her, swinging fast through the branches and vines, looking for shelter. Then the clouds burst violently open and rain came down in solid sheets, lashing down on to the trees with a noise like buckshot on an iron roof. Within seconds Alexa was soaked through. The rain poured off every leaf and branch and soon she was standing in a puddle that grew into a small pond.

The storm stopped as abruptly as it had started, leaving an unnatural stillness after the tumult of the rain. The sun came out again and everything began to steam, leaving the air dank and humid. Alexa pushed the wet hair off her face and moved on again, her feet squelching through the foul-smelling mud.

At every yard she expected to come face to face with a snake or jaguar or some other fearsome animal and walked in constant terror, but when she finally encountered her first living creature it turned out to be a man. A near-naked man with short cropped hair and black tribal markings on the brown skin of his

face. In his hands he carried a blowpipe and a large
bow, the arrows for it in a quiver slung across his
back. Alexa gave a cry of fright, but the Indian didn't
seem at all surprised to see her. She turned,
instinctively to run, remembered stories of cannibals
filling her mind, but when she did so found another
Indian behind her. So she stood still, trembling with
fear, her hands up to her face, too terrified even to
pray.

Other Indians came and they moved nearer,
talking softly among themselves. One reached forward with his bow and touched her and she gave a
cry of fear. They stood looking at her for a few
minutes then, until the same one spoke to her. Alexa
shook her head, desperately trying to control her
panic. At least they hadn't attacked her yet. Perhaps
they might even help her. She held out a hand in
appeal and the bracelet jingled on her wrist.
Immediately the Indians came closer and started
talking in their own language. Alexa tried one or two
words in Portuguese, but it was evident that they
didn't understand. They pointed at the bracelet,
making signs at her to take it off, but she drew back
reluctantly. Then the leader lunged forward to
snatch it roughly from her arm, making her cry out
in pain and fear. He gave it to another man, who
ran off with it back along the path, then the others
crowded round her, pushing her along between them.

They seemed to walk for a very long way, and once
the leader signalled and they all stood very still,
motioning Alexa to do the same. At first she couldn't
see why, but then, up in the branches caught sight of a
yellow spotted animal moving through the trees and
realised it was a jaguar. Fear kept her absolutely
motionless, even the Indians couldn't have frozen so

completely into the jungle, but they at least didn't feel afterwards as if their hearts had stopped.

At last they came to the Indian village in a clearing. Women and children, all quite naked, crowded round her, touching her hair and fingering her clothes, laughing and looking at her with wonder in their eyes. She suffered it, feeling deathly tired and afraid of what they were going to do with her now they had arrived. One of the women brought her a drink in a wooden bowl and she gulped it down thirstily even though it tasted foul. She nodded to the woman and smiled to show her thanks. Gradually they moved away and she looked round for somewhere to sit, but there was only the ground.

She wondered what Scott was doing. Whether he and the other men were searching for her. God, he must have been furious when he found that she'd wandered off! Alexa pictured his icy anger and shivered, but even that would be welcome if only he would come and find her. Uneasily she looked round the village of long, thatched huts. No one seemed to be taking much notice of her now; the men had mostly gone off again and the women were carrying on with their work, beating roots, cooking, or weaving leaves into mats. The sun was very hot on her head, making her feel dizzy. Alexa looked round for some shade, but there were only the long thatched houses. One of these was open-ended and she got up and went towards it. A young boy stood up as she entered and watched her curiously. It was very dark inside after the sunlight and it took her eyes some time to adjust. Over by the wall there was a thick coil of black rope that looked as if it would make a better seat than the ground. Alexa moved towards it and went to sit down, but the boy caught her arm and pulled her away. He pointed at the rope, said something and then kicked it with his foot. Slowly the top row of the coil started to unwind, then sway upwards, revealing itself to be the head of a snake. Alexa stood paralysed with shock as it slowly rose into the air weaving from side to side, then she screamed with pure terror and shot out of the hut faster than she had ever moved in her life.

Outside she grabbed hold of one of the women and pointed frantically back at the hut, gesticulating and trying to make her understand. Then suddenly the village seemed to sway around her before everything went black and she fell into a dead faint at the bewildered woman's feet.

CHAPTER SEVEN

WHEN Alexa came to, she moved as far away as possible from the hut where she had seen the snake. No one seemed at all worried by it, all the Indians going quite calmly about their business, several of them even going in and out of the house without any sign of alarm or fear on their faces. Alexa sat huddled on the ground facing the hut, her knees up under her chin and her arms wrapped round her legs, keeping her eyes fixed on the entrance so that she could get up and run if the snake came out. One of the women brought her some food, but she had visions of being fattened for the pot like a turkey for Christmas and couldn't eat it.

Her watch had stopped and she didn't know how long she had been sitting there, but it must have been for well over an hour before Alexa heard the Indians call out to one another and saw them move towards one end of the village where a narrow trail entered the forest. Dully she looked after them, her emotions too numbed to be afraid of some new threat. An Indian came into the village followed by a man wearing cheap working clothes, and behind him . . .! Alexa leapt to her feet and ran towards them. 'Scott! Oh, Scott!'

She ran to him and threw her arms round his neck, holding him so tightly that he could hardly breathe, her hands locked together as if she was afraid someone would tear her from him. His arms came round her, strong and comforting, and it was the most wonderful feeling she'd ever known. For several minutes she could only cling to him, sobbing incoherently and saying his name over and over again.

'Easy—easy now! You're safe, Alexa. You're safe now.'

He said other things, too, words of comfort, but she was weeping her relief and fear out on his shoulder and didn't hear the actual words, only felt the tone of reassurance and the warmth and security of his arms. He let her cry for a few minutes, then gently put up a hand to push the tangled hair from her dirt-streaked face.

'Hush now! Everything's going to be okay.'

Alexa nodded and tried to smile, but her body was still shaking and she kept her hands tight around his neck. 'How did you—how did you find me?'

With his thumb, Scott wiped the tears from her cheeks. 'One of the Indians came to the camp to tell us where you were. He brought your bracelet to show us.' He grinned at her. 'Didn't I tell you it would bring you luck?'

She laughed shakily and nodded, then her face grew serious again. 'I was so scared! And then the Indians found me and I was afraid they might eat me. Oh, Scott, I'm glad you came! I'm so glad you came!' And she clung to him tightly again.

He gave a shout of laughter. 'You crazy little idiot! These Indians haven't eaten people for hundreds of years.' But his arms tightened round her and he held her close, her head against his shoulder.

An Indian, the one who seemed to be the leader, came up to them and spoke to the Brazilian who was acting as interpreter.

'The Indians wish us to drink with them,' he told Scott in Portuguese.

Two women brought up wooden bowls of the milky

white liquid that they had given Alexa, but the men got far more smiles and ceremonial bows than she had had. Evidently here, too, women were definitely second class citizens.

'It's horrible. They gave me some,' Alexa warned.

'I know, but it's a drink they offer all strangers to their village. It would be very rude to refuse it.' He drank and handed back the bowl with a smile. 'Maybe one day I'll tell you how they make it.'

Alexa shuddered and he put his arm round her again, but her tremors had largely quietened now. 'Feeling better?'

She nodded and managed a smile. 'I'm sorry, I'm afraid I soaked your shirt.'

'It'll dry.' His eyes settled on her face. 'You know, you deserve to be put over my knee and given a good spanking for wandering off like that!'

'I don't know how I came to get lost. One minute I was in sight and sound of the camp and the next I was completely lost with jungle all around me.'

'It happens. We searched for you all around the camp and found the flowers that you'd dropped. If you'd stayed put we would have found you quite soon, but you kept pushing deeper and deeper into the jungle.'

'I thought I was going back towards the camp. I was afraid to stand still in case a snake found me.' She suddenly grew rigid and gripped his arm agitatedly, her nails digging into his flesh. 'The snake! Oh God, I forgot. Scott, there's a snake here—over in that hut. It was all coiled up and I nearly sat on it. I tried to tell them, but nobody will take any notice of me.'

Scott turned to the Brazilian, who spoke in turn to one of the Indians, then the answer was relayed back. 'They say it's only a boa-constrictor,' Scott explained.

Alexa's voice rose incredulously. '*Only* a boa-constrictor! My God, what's that supposed to mean?'

His mouth curled in amusement. 'The Indians often keep one around the place as a pet. They keep the village free of rats and mice. And if they ever get short of food the Indians can always eat the snake; I'm told they taste very good, like chicken.'

The thought made Alexa feel sick. She remembered the bowl of food the Indian woman had brought her and was deeply grateful that she hadn't eaten it. 'Do you think we could go back to the camp now?' she asked faintly.

Scott looked at her white face and nodded. 'But first we'd better give the chief some presents for finding you.'

Alexa noticed now that he had carried the box of supplies with him and he proceeded to hand them out, the Indians crowding round and talking excitedly over each new thing that came out of the box like children round Father Christmas. Scott made the Brazilian workman carefully explain how the medicines were to be used, but the Indians seemed to be far more interested in the bags of salt he gave them, and which Scott explained were like gold dust this far up the Amazon basin.

The chief came over and held out the charm bracelet to her, rather reluctantly, Alexa thought. She looked at Scott questioningly. 'Does he want it? Would it be all right if I give it to him?'

'Of course. Try him?'

Tentatively Alexa held out the bracelet, making signs for the man to take it. He gave a big smile and placed it on his arm, waving it about so that all the tribe could see and hear it jingle.

They left soon after, an Indian leading the way,

followed by the Brazilian interpreter, then Alexa and Scott bringing up the rear. They went along a path much like the one Alexa had followed, the Indian picking his way surely along despite his bare feet. Once or twice they stopped for nothing that Alexa could see, and she felt Scott move up closer behind her, his hand on the gun he had got stuck into his belt, but after a couple of miles of trekking through the jungle they arrived safely at the camp.

The Brazilian labourers crowded round, wanting to know what had happened, but Scott led her firmly over to a hut that was used as a wash-house. 'You can shower in here. I'll see if I can find you some clean clothes.'

Obediently Alexa stripped off her things and stepped into one of the cubicles. There was some rather harsh soap which would have to do for both her body and hair, but it felt good to wash away the dirt and sweat of the jungle. She soaped herself energetically all over, scrubbing herself clean again.

'Here's a towel for you.'

'Thanks.' Alexa turned off the water and took the big, rough towel that Scott had hung on the partition wall. She rubbed herself dry, then wrapped it round her and stepped out.

Scott was waiting; his eyes ran over her and he said, 'You need another towel for your hair. Here, let me rub it for you.' He picked up a smaller towel and draped it over her hair, then began to vigorously rub it dry, one hand on either side of her head.

'Hey!' Alexa laughed and lifted her head, her hair in a dark mass round her face. 'Not so hard, you'll knock my head off!'

His hands slowed and then grew still, although he still held them on either side of her head. His grey eyes searched her face intently, then darkened as his hands tightened. Alexa gazed back at him, her lips slowly parting, the bottom one full and sensuous. Scott drew in his breath sharply, he moved towards her and her heart seemed to stand still for a minute as she thought that he was going to kiss her. But then he made an explosive sound deep in his throat and jerked away from her, letting the towel fall from his hands.

Turning abruptly away, he said harshly, 'I've found you a pair of jeans and a shirt that belong to one of the smaller men, but they'll have to do. Your underthings are okay, aren't they?' he asked, looking down at her discarded pants and bra.

'Yes. They're fine.' She said it slowly, looking at his broad back, but he didn't turn round again, just nodded and walked away.

Picking up the towel, Alexa went on drying her hair, but her movements had lost their former energy and she did it automatically. She stared at the door, her thoughts full of that look on Scott's face. She had seen that look once before, on the night she had met him, when he had been about to make love to her. And she was sure, now, that he had been going to kiss her. But something had made him stop, pull back, and she could only think that it must have been his promise, made back in England, that he wouldn't touch her. Her hands shaking, Alexa began to dress. The clothes fitted quite well, they would do. Scott had brought her bag for her and she went over to the large but rather chipped mirror and began to comb her hair.

Her hand stopped as she stared at her reflection; had she wanted him to kiss her? If he had would she have tried to stop him? Well, of course she would; she was in love with his brother, wasn't she? No, I'm not. Her reflection seemed to say the words back to her, quite definitely and firmly. It was something she hadn't admitted to herself even when she had put Mark's photograph away in the drawer, because until now she hadn't had to face up to the fact that Scott had taken his place. So thoroughly that she couldn't remember the last time she had grieved over Mark, had yearned for him. She hadn't even thought about him lately and could only remember what he looked like because he was so like Scott. The complete reversal of feeling took her breath away. How could she possibly have fallen out of love with one man and in love with another so quickly? The answer could only be that she had never really loved Mark. But she had thought that she loved him, had been quite sure of it, and wanted to die when he married Elaine. So how could she possibly be sure that she loved Scott? Perhaps it wasn't love at all. Perhaps it was just because he was around all the time, living in such close proximity. Perhaps it was just sex or frustration, the need for a man.

Alexa put her hands up to her temples, her mind in a whirl. She was suddenly, savagely glad that he hadn't kissed her, because now she didn't have to make any decisions. Fiercely she finished doing her hair, dragging the comb through the tangles, then applied some lipstick and threw the things back in the bag, her hands shaking.

It was almost dark when she went outside, the sun on the point of setting. Scott was talking to the head forester, but he came over when he saw her.

'I'm ready to go. Where's the helicopter?' she asked, looking round.

'It had to leave earlier so that it could get back before dark. The pilot hung on until he knew you were safe and then took the technicians back.'

'Well, when is it coming to pick us up?'

'Not until tomorrow morning. They won't risk flying over the jungle at night.'

Alexa looked at him in dismay. 'You mean we have to stay here all night?'

'Afraid so. It won't be as luxurious as the bungalow, but they'll do their best to make us comfortable,' he added dryly.

She flushed. 'Yes, I'm sure they will. It—it wasn't that.'

'No? What, then?'

But she shook her head and looked away avoiding his eyes. 'Oh, nothing really. I would just have been glad to go home.' Home where she felt safe, strangely enough, even though they would be alone in the bungalow together.

'There's a meal ready in the dining-hut.'

The men had, as he'd said, done their best, smartening themselves up and putting on a good meal which had more quantity than quality. Tins of beer were consumed at a rapid rate and there was much teasing of the poor man whose clothes Alexa had borrowed, most of which she couldn't understand but definitely got the drift. There wasn't anything else to drink, so she had to have beer too, although she didn't like the bitter taste very much, but it grew on you after a while. Brazilians need little or no excuse for a party, so after the meal one of the men brought out an old accordion and another a whistle and they played some folk tunes, then another joined in on an improvised drum and they played samba music which some of the others danced to. They finished off the evening with something called the *capoeira*, which looked more like a karate kicking exhibition than a dance but was received with great applause and whistles by the rest of the men.

When the party broke up it was pitch black and too early for the moon. The others very courteously stayed behind while Scott took a torch and guided Alexa over to the wash-hut, checking it first to make sure no snakes had crawled in to keep cool. When she came out he took her arm and led her over to a small hut standing a little apart from the others. Opening the door, he switched on the light.

'This is the head forester's hut, but he's given it over to us for tonight.'

The hut was unpainted and there were darker squares on the walls where pin-up pictures had been hurriedly taken down. It was sparsely furnished with a desk, table and chair, wardrobe and a single bed. Another camp bed had been made up and stood alongside it. Alexa looked at the two beds and stiffened.

'We both have to sleep in here?'

'You could hardly expect them to give us separate rooms. There's only limited accommodation at the camp.'

'You could go and sleep in with the men.'

A frown of anger crossed his face. 'If you're so against sleeping in the same room as me, then *you* go over and sleep with the men, because I'm not.' Sitting down on the edge of the camp bed, he began to take off his shoes. Alexa stood looking at him uncertainly until he said exasperatedly, 'For heaven's sake, woman, get undressed and go to bed. This is no different from the bungalow; we haven't got a wall between us, that's all.'

He spoke as if the lack of a wall was nothing, but Alexa wasn't so sure, not after the way he had looked at her earlier. She had been aware of him beside her all evening, of their hips touching as they sat on the

bench, of his shoulder against hers, and the casual way
he had put a hand on her shoulder when it had been
time to go.

'Now what is it?' he demanded as she still stood
unmoving.

'There aren't any curtains.'

'Picking a blanket up off his bed, Scott went across
and hooked it across the window. 'That do?'

'Yes. Thanks.'

Turning her back on him, Alexa kicked off her
shoes, then pulled off her sweater. She hesitated a
moment, wondering if he was watching her or had
turned away, but she was afraid to look. Unzipping
the jeans, she quickly wriggled out of them and
dropped them on the end of the bed, the shirt long
enough to fall down over her hips. With trembling
fingers she unbuttoned it, then hastily pulled it off and
dived into bed in her underwear. Stealing a glance at
Scott, she saw that he was quite unconcernedly
stripping down to his pants.

'Ready?'

She nodded and he padded over to switch off the
light. The bed creaked as he got into it. 'Goodnight,
Alexa.'

' 'Night!'

Turning over on to her side, Alexa laughed at
herself with some relief. It was silly of her to have
been scared; she knew she could trust Scott: hadn't he
come to find her in the jungle? She yawned sleepily.
'Scott?'

'Mm?'

'Wasn't it lucky that the Indians found me in the
forest? It must have been the good luck charm
working overtime.'

'Hardly,' Scott answered dryly. 'They told us you

made as much noise as a herd of wild pigs charging through the jungle.'

'Well, really! Of all the cheek! I bet . . .'

'Alexa—go to sleep.'

She chuckled, her uneasiness forgotten, and soon obeyed him.

It was some time later and she was moving restlessly in her sleep, dreaming of being lost again, of being cold and wet. She could see the thatched Indian house where the snake was in the distance and she kept getting nearer and nearer to it even though she tried not to. Suddenly, from outside, there came a bloodcurdling scream. Alexa sat up, her nerves on edge, hot and sticky with sweat, her body trembling. For a moment she thought that the scream had been in her dream, that she might even have uttered it herself, but then it came again, shattering the silence, making her hair stand on end.

Leaping out of bed, Alexa grabbed hold of Scott and began to shake him. 'Wake up! Oh, please wake up!'

'What is it?' He sat up, instantly alert, catching hold of her arms.

'Listen! Someone's being murdered out there. It sounds as if they're being torn to pieces. Perhaps a jaguar or something has got into the camp, has taken one of the men.' She pulled at him agitatedly as she spoke, wanting him to get up and go and see. 'There it is again!'

For a third time the scream split the night and she felt Scott's grip relax. 'It's all right.' His hands came up to cover hers. 'It's only a howler monkey. They always scream like that during the night. They start the other animals off and you'll hear them all soon.'

'A monkey? That's all it was? Are you sure?'

'Quite sure.' Scott's hands tightened. 'You're

shivering with cold. Here, come and get warm for a minute.'

He moved over in the narrow bed and, after only a slight hesitation, Alexa got in beside him, glad of his warmth. 'Just for a minute, then.'

He put his left arm under her head because there wasn't room to put it anywhere else and she moved an inch or two nearer, her head against his shoulder. For a few moments they lay in silence listening to the sounds of the jungle outside. Alexa shivered again and Scott began to gently stroke her arm. His hand was so firm and strong, and so warm on her bare skin. She gave a murmur of pleasure and his hand stilled for a moment then moved on to her shoulder and her neck, pushing her bra strap aside. Scott moved slightly and his body touched hers along its length. His skin felt burning hot. His hand was caressing her throat, moving on down.

'I—I think I'm warm again now.'

She went to move away, but he stopped her. 'No, don't go.' His voice sounded hoarse, strange.

'Scott, I . . .'

But then his lips were on hers, soft, exploring, and he was half lying on her, pinning her down with the weight of his body. For a few minutes she resisted him, her mouth closed tight against his kiss, but immediately his lips became hard and compelling, bruising her as he demanded her submission. Deep down she felt the rise of sensuality, a feeling that grew until her body began to burn with heat. Slowly her lips parted and her senses reeled as his mouth took possession, forcing her to respond with growing passion.

Scott pulled himself up on his elbow and his hand went to the hook of her bra, undoing it and pulling it off. Then his hand was on her breasts, cupping their soft firmness, creating waves of pleasure that made her nipples harden under his caressing fingers. His mouth came down again to gently brush her lips and then move on, touching lightly on her throat and across the white mounds of her breasts. Alexa gasped, her hands twined in his hair. She moved her legs against him, loving the touch of his skin against her own. His hands moved to her waist, caressing its deep curve, then on down to her hips. Finding the top of her pants, he began to gently pull them down.

She tried to oppose him then, but desire and excitement had weakened her resistance and his mouth and hands were too knowledgeable and experienced. They moved over her, waking her body to a new awareness, arousing pleasure that she didn't know existed. She relaxed and he explored her nakedness at his leisure while Alexa's body arched towards him, greedy for the ecstasy his hands and mouth could give her.

'Alexa.' His voice was thick and unsteady. 'God, how I want you!'

His hands were burning hot on her body, like fingers of fire running over her. Her lips were against his shoulder, tasting the hot salt taste of the perspiration that glowed on his skin. She could feel the hardness of his body pressing against her through the thin cotton of his pants. Digging her nails into him, she moved her hips against his until he groaned and grabbed her shoulders, kissing her so fiercely that he bent her head back into the pillows. She wanted him now, wanted him so badly, her whole body cried out to be loved. Her breath came in hot, ragged gasps. Alexa pressed herself against him, her body urgent with need, but still he held back. Her mind went back

to the last time when they had been in bed together
and she had spoilt everything by calling him Mark.
Was that why he was holding back? Was he afraid she
was still making believe he was another man?

Moving her head to one side, Alexa put her arms
round his neck and gently bit his ear. He gasped and
his hand tightened on her waist. 'Scott,' she
whispered.

'Yes?' The word was more of a groan.

'I—I just wanted you to know that—that I know it's
you, and not Mark.'

His body grew tense and his hands gripped her so
hard that it hurt. 'Did you go to bed with him? Did
you?' The question came out on a note of harsh
interrogation and she realised then why he had been
holding back. Sudden red-hot rage filled her and she
pushed him violently away, swinging herself out of
bed before he could stop her.

Then she turned on him. 'That's all you care about,
isn't it? Every time we have a row you ask the same
questions. Have I been to bed with Mark? Has he ever
made love to me? What is it with you—some kind of
obsession?' she yelled.

Scott rolled out of bed, moved across to the window
and jerked aside the blanket so that the room was
flooded with moonlight and he could see her. That it
also revealed her nakedness, Alexa was too angry to
care.

'Well, what is it with you?' she yelled again. 'Have
you got some crazy hang-up about Mark? What does it
matter whether I've slept with him or not?'

Scott took two swift strides and caught her by the
wrists, his face angrier than she'd ever seen it. 'It
matters,' he snarled. 'My God, it matters!'

'Why? Because you're too fastidious to take your

brother's leavings?' Alexa struggled and managed to get one hand free. She hit him across the face with it with all the strength in her arm, shouting, 'Well, you'll never know, will you?'

'You bitch! I'm going to make you tell me.'

He tried to catch her arm, but she flailed out at him, using her nails as claws and trying to knee him, her fury giving her strength and complete disregard for anything he might do to her in return.

Scott swore explosively as her nails raked his chest, his hands slipping on the moist skin of her arm as he tried to recapture it. 'Damn you, tell me the truth!' He jerked her off balance suddenly and grabbed her, holding her squirming and struggling against his almost naked body. After a few minutes, as his arms slowly tightened against her struggles, Alexa knew that she hadn't the strength to break free again and that it wouldn't be any good even if she did. Her breath dry and panting in her throat, she gasped out, 'All right, if you want to know so badly, then I'll tell you.' His arms relaxed and he slowly let her go, his dark eyes fixed intently on her face as if trying to analyse her every change of expression.

'You want to know if I ever went to bed with Mark.' She paused, watching him, seeing the tension in his shoulders, in his clenched fists. 'Well, the answer's yes! Yes, do you hear me? I went to bed with him not once but dozens of times! And Elaine was right, he is a wonderful lover. I let him do anything he wanted to me. Anything at all. And compared to him you're just a schoolboy, a rank amateur, and . . .'

Scott suddenly exploded into movement. He had been standing very still, but now he leapt at her, his face savage with fury. Alexa cried out once, but then she was borne backwards and thrown roughly down on to her own bed. His voice shaking with uncontrollable rage, Scott shouted, 'You little slut! My God, I'll show you whether I'm a schoolboy or not! I'll show you just what you've been missing with my little brother!' And then he came down upon her, his face twisted with murderous anger.

He took her in a blaze of savagery, and only afterwards realised why it had been so difficult, why Alexa had cried out in pain. He lay beside her, his chest heaving, and put up a hand to wipe away her tears. 'You lied. You've never been to bed with a man before. Dear God, Alexa, why did you lie to me? Why didn't you tell me it was the first time?'

She didn't answer, just turned her torn, trembling body so that she lay with her back to him.

'Alexa?' His hand came up to cover her shoulder and a violent shudder ran through her. Gently he began to stroke her hair, easing it back from where it clung damply to her face. 'I didn't mean to hurt you. If only you'd told me the truth . . .'

He went on stroking her hair for some time, talking to her quietly and gradually feeling her tremors die away, then he firmly turned her over on to her back. 'Alexa, listen to me. I . . .' He went to go on, but the blanket had fallen down below her waist and the moonlight lay across her, creating shadows that played around the peaks and valleys of her breasts, across the hollow of her waist and the taut smoothness of her stomach. His voice caught in his throat and his eyes darkened with desire. Almost of its own accord, his hand reached out to draw the blanket completely aside.

'Oh God, Alexa, you're so lovely,' he murmured, his voice thick and unsteady.

His hands began to stroke and caress her and she lay

still, letting him do what he wanted, gazing up at the twisting patterns of light on the ceiling. But then her breathing quickened and she gasped as his hands found places that sent waves of sensuality coursing through her body. She reached out and began to explore in her turn, tentatively at first, but then with growing confidence as she felt his body tense and he said her name on a note of wonder and delight. They kissed, hungrily, devouringly, and then his lips and hands moved over her, setting her body on fire so that when he took her again she cried out with joy and held him close, never wanting to part.

His mouth was on hers, gasping, speaking unintelligibly against her lips, then he moved and she heard the harsh intake of his breath, which changed to a thick groan as his body surged with pleasure. As it heightened he cried out her name, but she was too lost to hear, lost in the closeness of their bodies and the ecstasy that only love can bring.

'Alexa. Oh, God! Oh, darling!' For some time he couldn't speak, but then Scott turned to her, his voice hoarse and broken and drew her close to him, holding her tenderly. Alexa didn't answer but smiled contentedly in the darkness and snuggled against him, falling almost instantly asleep.

It was light when she awoke, the sunlight pouring into the hut and turning the white walls to gold. Alexa opened her eyes and felt as if she had come into a brand new, beautiful world. She wanted to shout and sing with happiness. She ran her hands down her body, wondering if it showed that she was a woman, wondering if she looked any different. Tentatively she moved in the bed, but found that she was alone. Sitting up, she looked across at the camp-bed, but that, too, was empty; Scott must have dressed and gone out quietly so as not to wake her. Alexa lay down again, a smug, contented smile on her face. So that was what love was like! Well, Scott had certainly made good his word; he was most definitely a man and not a schoolboy, as she'd taunted him. And now she had no need to be envious of Elaine.

A sudden sadness filled her, huge and overwhelming. If only she'd met Scott first instead of Mark! If only she hadn't made such a fool of herself when she had met him. Or even realised sooner that she loved him. They'd wasted so much time that they would never have again. And she'd been so stupid not to realise it. But thank God it wasn't too late! Thank God that last night they had come together at last. And so very, very rapturously. Emotion swelled her heart and became too much for her. Alexa turned her head into the pillow and wept tears of mingled sorrow and relief, but most of all of infinite happiness and gratitude.

CHAPTER EIGHT

'ALEXA—breakfast!'

Scott's voice carried through the closed door, and she quickly finished putting on her lipstick, tossing her things back in the bag and hurrying to join him. But when she opened the door Alexa saw that he was already half-way back to the dining-hut. She ran to catch him up, but the head forester joined them just as she did so.

'Morning, Scott. Morning, Mrs Kelsey. I trust you haven't suffered any ill effects from your adventure yesterday?'

'No, I'm fine, thank you.' She looked towards Scott as she spoke, her eyes brilliant, wanting him to turn and look at her so that she could smile at him, show him how happy she was. And she wanted to see his face, to see the look in his eyes that would be only for her: the warm, private acknowledgement of their shared secret. But he didn't look directly at her, just held the door open and made some remark to the forester.

She slid along one of the benches on either side of the long table, expecting Scott to slide in beside her, but somehow there was a mix-up and, to her sharp disappointment, the head forester sat next to her instead, Scott sitting on his other side so that she couldn't even see him properly. Breakfast seemed to take an age. Alexa had no idea what was put in front of her, she certainly didn't eat much of it because her stomach was churning with a crazy kind of excitement.

She longed to be alone with Scott, to touch him and to feel the warmth of his hand on her arm. Why, he hadn't even kissed her good morning yet.

At last breakfast was over and they heard the sound of the helicopter approaching. Alexa ran to collect her sweater and dirty clothes and then said goodbye to all the friendly workers at the camp, receiving many invitations to come again soon. One of them, the Brazilian who had acted as interpreter with the Indians even came forward with a huge grin and presented her with a big bunch of orchids to replace the ones she had lost in the jungle.

Alexa thanked him with a dazzling smile and turned back to wave as she hurried after Scott, who was already walking the hundred yards or so to where the helicopter had touched down and was waiting for them. Catching up with him, she said rather breathlessly, 'Wasn't it kind of him to pick these for me?'

'Yes, very,' Scott agreed abruptly. 'We'd better hurry. I've a lot of work to do and I want to get back to the office as soon as possible.'

His tone was cold, as cold as his face when Alexa looked at him. There was no warmth in his eyes, no tenderness in his voice. Nothing there that she had expected to see. Just a withdrawn remoteness as if she was some chance acquaintance who was rather a nuisance. Ducking under the rotor blades, he opened the door for her but didn't offer to help her inside.

Alexa sat in her seat and rather tremblingly did up her safety strap. Scott climbed in beside her and she looked at him searchingly, a tentative smile hovering on her lips, unable to believe that he was acting so strangely, thinking that perhaps he hadn't wanted to show his feelings in front of the men at the camp. For a moment, as he sat down, he looked towards her and Alexa's heart flared with anticipation, but then his glance moved on, completely impassive, and when his hand happened to touch hers as he did up his safety strap, he immediately moved it out of the way and made no attempt to maintain the contact.

Shaken, she sat back in her seat, her fingers gripping the arms tightly. Why was he behaving like this? What had she done? Biting back tears, Alexa let her mind go back over last night, trying to think of anything that could possibly have led to his coldness this morning. Was it because she'd lied to him about Mark? He'd been angry then, terribly angry. So furious that he'd completely lost control of his emotions and taken her whether she was willing or not. Although she had been willing enough, had goaded him in fact to doing just that because he had made her feel guilty for having loved Mark and afraid that it would come between them. She hadn't wanted Mark to come between them that night and her sense of guilt had made her lash out and hurt Scott for holding back, for caring whether or not she had been to bed with his brother. But her lies had lit such a flame of raw savagery in him that she had been carried along and engulfed by it.

And afterwards? When he had found out that she had never been loved by Mark or any man before? Then he'd been tender, so exquisitely tender and loving, so that when again he made love to her it had been the most wonderfully sensuous experience of her life. And she had been so sure that he had felt the same, that he, too, had been carried along on a great wave of sensuality that had lifted them both to the heights of passion and fulfilment.

But this morning he was like some stranger. No, not

some stranger; like a man who actively disliked her
and wanted nothing more to do with her. So what was
she supposed to think? The only answer that came into
her mind was so abhorrent that she immediately thrust
it aside, but as the helicopter ride came to an end and
they transferred to a train, and still Scott remained
aloof and cold, the thought came back and was
reluctantly accepted: Scott had taken what he wanted
and was no longer interested.

Not once had it ever occurred to her that he might
be that type of man and she found it almost impossible
to believe now. But why else was he treating her like
this? A great sadness filled her and Alexa turned to
stare out of the window, gazing unseeingly at the
serried ranks of tree plantations that stretched to the
far horizon. Her eyes pricked and she had to bite her
lip hard to stop herself bursting into tears. Her hands
were balled into tight fists, her nails digging into her
palms. Scott sat beside her, reading a Brazilian
newspaper, apparently impervious to her distress.
Suddenly she wanted to turn on him and tear the
paper away, to hit out at him and claw at his face with
her nails until she drew blood. But there were other
people in the carriage, men travelling to Monte
Dourado to visit their families, and one didn't lose
control and make a scene like that in public.

Alexa leant back against the seat and closed her
eyes, her face white beneath her tan. He could at least
speak to her. He must know that she was in an
emotional turmoil after last night. After all, it wasn't
every day that one lost one's virginity! It occurred to
her suddenly that he might be ashamed of what he'd
done, regret that he had taken her in anger with
masculine violence. But Scott wasn't the kind of man
ever to be ashamed of his actions; regret them, maybe.

But man enough to put them behind him and live for the present. Or at least she had always thought so, but now she wasn't sure of anything any more. She gazed miserably out of the window, wondering if she ought to make some sort of approach, tell him how she felt. But then she remembered how sure of himself he had been the second time he had made love to her and knew that shame hadn't come into the picture at all. He had taken her because he wanted her and would never, ever regret it—even though he now seemed to despise her because of it.

When they got to Monte Dourado, Scott brusquely suggested that she get a taxi to take her home as he wanted to take the car and go straight to the office. The way he said it, it might just as well have been a straight out order. Alexa, her face drained of colour, stared at him stonily for a moment, then gave a brief nod and strode towards the taxi rank without looking back, her heart feeling as if it was breaking for the second time.

Luckily Maria was out shopping when she got home, so Alexa was able to close the door behind her and thank God that she was alone at last. She leaned against the wall, but her legs buckled under her and she slid down to the floor. She sat there for a very long time, too numb to cry, just gazing blindly at the opposite wall. Her borrowed clothing penetrated her vision and she knew that she ought to go and change, but her limbs felt as if every last drop of strength had been drained out of them, and it was only the sight of the wilting orchids, still clutched in her hand, that made her at last stir and drag herself into movement.

When Scott came home that night he found her dressed ready to go out for the evening, her face pale under rather heavy make-up and her eyes unnaturally bright.

'Hi,' she greeted him as soon as he came in. 'Maria wanted the evening off, so I said we'd eat at the Club. That's okay with you, isn't it?'

'Sure, I'll go and change.' His eyes rested on her for a moment, but Alexa turned away.

'I'll mix you up a cocktail,' she told him with false vivacity. 'It's a new recipe I made up myself. I'm calling it the Brazilian Bombshell.'

'Sounds great. I'll be right out.'

He went into his bedroom and closed the door and Alexa slumped into a chair. Oh God, she couldn't stand any more! Not to have loved and lost both of them. Anything but that!

Somehow she managed to compose herself before he came out and handed him a tall cocktail glass. 'Here, try it.'

Scott sipped experimentally, felt the spirits hit the back of his throat and said, 'Good grief! What have you put in these?'

'You shouldn't ask that. Just drink it and enjoy it. Knowing what's in it spoils half the fun.' Finishing off her own drink, she poured herself another, filling the glass to the brim.

'How many of these have you had?' he asked her casually, his eyes on her face.

She gave a brittle laugh. 'You can hardly expect me to invent a new cocktail without tasting it, now can you? What do you think of the name? The Brazilian Bombshell. Or perhaps you think it too trite?' Without waiting for him to speak she swept on, 'I know, perhaps I'll call it after me. Bloody Alexa instead of Bloody Mary.' For a second her voice broke, but she covered it by swallowing down her drink and saying impatiently, 'Oh, come on, let's go. I'm starving!'

But although she claimed to be hungry, Alexa hardly touched her food. She was very animated all evening, greeting everyone they knew exuberantly, laughing loudly, drinking a lot, and pulling the men in the crowd up on the floor to dance with her. Once or twice she danced with Scott, but she made sure they were fast beat numbers where they danced far apart. And she really let herself go that night, moving with primitive rhythm, her hair swirling round her head, her red dress clinging to her as she swayed and gyrated to the music with complete abandon.

Once she looked up and saw Scott walk across to speak to Patti Jordan. The other girl turned to him and his face lit in a smile, his hands going out to clasp hers. A great surge of jealousy stabbed like a knife into Alexa's heart. Stabbed and turned again and again. There was a glass of whisky in front of her and she drank it down in one gulp. There was also a pack of cigarettes belonging to Chris Anderson. 'Mind if I try one of these?' she asked him, and held it with shaking fingers towards the light he offered her.

The cigarette made her choke at first. She gasped and her eyes watered.

'Haven't you ever smoked before?' Chris asked her.

'No, this is my very first one.' She gave a high, unnatural laugh. 'But then I'm trying out a whole lot of new things for the very first time today.'

It was late when they left the Club: Alexa refusing to leave until the very end. They drove home in silence, Scott grim-faced, Alexa leaning back against the seat, her head rolling with the movement of the car. When they got home, she staggered going up the step and Scott put out a hand to steady her, but she snatched her arm away, sending herself off balance and only saving herself from falling by a lucky grab at the doorjamb. Scott put on the light and she marched unsteadily ahead of him into the sitting-room, throwing her bag and stole on to a chair and going over to the drinks cabinet to pour herself out a whisky.

'You've had enough of that.' Scott's hand came over hers and took the decanter away.

'Give it back to me! I want a drink.'

'I said you've had enough.'

Alexa glared at him. She felt so strange, like two different people. But the pain had gone, the hurt numbed by alcohol. 'All right, so I'll drink something else.' Angrily she turned back to the cabinet and grabbed a bottle at random.

'Alexa, stop this!' Scott twisted the bottle from her grip, then caught her wrists and pulled her away. 'Look, I want to talk to you.' He hesitated, then said, 'About last night . . .'

Alexa's laugh rang out, bitter and hysterical. 'Oh, you do remember that there was a last night, then?'

His grip tightened and a bleak, fed-up look came into Scott's eyes. For a moment he looked as if he was about to make some hasty remark, but he bit it back and said harshly, 'I just wanted to say that you don't have to be afraid. It won't happen again.'

Her body shook beneath his hands and her eyes closed tight shut in pain. Almost she cried out, but then her eyes, alight with fury, opened again and she pulled free of his hold. But she didn't yell or shout, instead turning on him in cold, tight-lipped anger. 'You're right. It won't happen again—ever. Because if you ever lay a finger on me again, I'll kill you! I swear I'll kill you!' Then she turned and strode into her bedroom, the alcohol no longer strong enough to dull the agony that tore through her heart.

It was very late when she woke the next day, and it felt as if someone was trying to hammer nails into her head. Maria prepared lunch for her, but Alexa pushed it aside and helped herself to another drink, swallowing it down with a couple of aspirins which dulled the hammer blows to constant drumbeats. She dressed and drove to the Club, calling on the way at the supermarket where she bought herself a twenty pack carton of American cigarettes and a lighter. They were playing bridge at the Club and she made up a four with some women she hadn't played with before. They suggested making the game more interesting by playing for money and Alexa enthusiastically accepted. She called the waiter over and ordered a round of drinks, lit up a cigarette and settled down for the afternoon. When the game broke up a few hours later she had lost over two hundred American dollars and was so tight that she drove home as wildly as any Brazilian, hacking a large gouge out of the gatepost as she came in. Then she collapsed on the bed, slept for an hour and woke in time to get ready and demand that Scott take her to the Club again.

She went on in the same way for nearly a week, sleeping till gone lunchtime then going to the Club to drink. Scott had stopped coming home for lunch so she was able to keep it from him, but then, driving back from the Club one afternoon, she swerved to avoid another car, went off the road and crashed into a tree. She wasn't hurt, but it was obvious to the policeman who came along that she had been drinking, so he took her home and sent for Scott. He pulled into the driveway with a screech of brakes and ran in to find Alexa half lying on the settee, a glass in one hand and a cigarette in the other.

'Are you all right? What the hell happened?'

Alexa opened dull eyes and gave him a fuddled smile. 'Hi there, Scott, old man. How's Britain's answer to Casanova this fine morning? Or is it afternoon? I lost count.'

His eyes widened in growing awareness and he suddenly bent down and snatched the glass from her. 'How many of these have you had? Answer me!' he demanded. 'How many drinks have you had?'

'Who the hell's counting? Do you have to shout?' Alexa frowned, her head aching and reaching up a hand for the drink. 'Give it back to me—I need it. I had a liddle accident in the car.'

'A little accident!' Scott exclaimed disgustedly. 'The car's smashed in all down one side—I saw it on my way over here.'

'It's these mad Brazilians. They drive on the wrong side of the road. Did you know that? And they won't get out of the way when you—when you sound the horn at them.' She pulled on her cigarette, but suddenly had it twitched from her fingers and pitched out of the open window. Then Scott pulled her roughly to her feet. But she couldn't stand by herself and began to reel so that he had to hold her up. 'Were you drinking before you had the accident?'

She gave him a slack smile. 'Might have had a liddle drink or two to keep the cold out.' Then she began to giggle. 'But it isn't cold in Brazil, is it? Very hot in Brazil.' Suddenly her face changed and her eyes focussed on him properly. 'So why do I always feel so cold inside, Scott?' she said in little more than a despairing whisper. 'Why am I so icy cold inside?'

He stared back at her, his face tense and pale. Almost under his breath he muttered, 'Oh God, Alexa, what the hell have I done to you?'

But she didn't hear because she'd begun to cry with big, noisy sobs, and he swiftly put an arm under her legs and picked her up, carrying her into her room where he laid her on the bed. Then he gently took off her shoes and pulled the covers over her, watching grimly as she almost immediately fell into a troubled sleep.

When Alexa eventually woke the next day and went in search of a drink to cure her hangover, she found that all the booze had disappeared, together with her cigarettes. Her car keys and money were also missing from her bag. For some time, she just rampaged through the house, unable to eat, or even to sit still, her head pounding and her throat dry as dust. She snapped at Maria when the maid offered her a cold drink and was immediately sorry for it. A book didn't even hold her interest for the first page. It was too hot to walk outside and she had no means of transport to get her to the Club and not even the money to pay for a taxi.

By the time Scott got home that evening she was in a flaming temper and picked up a heavy glass ashtray the moment she heard his key in the door. When he walked into the sitting-room, she threw it as hard as she could at his head. Luckily for him he ducked and the ashtray went through the doorway and smashed against the wall, but the vase she followed up with caught him on the shoulder and he hastily put up a hand to protect his face from the barrage of objects she had ready to hand.

'For God's sake, Alexa!' Springing across the room, he caught hold of her and pinned her arms to her sides, then twisted her right wrist until she dropped the solid brass ornament that was to have been the next item to throw at his head.

Alexa tried to struggle free, kicking him and trying to butt him with her head, but he held her squirming body in a vicelike grip. She started to swear at him, panting, tears of anger and frustration running down her cheeks.

'You swine! You louse! Let me go—do you hear me? Let go of me!'

'Why, so that you can claw my eyes out?' His grip tightened as she exerted all her strength to break free. 'Be still, damn you!'

At last she gave up and stood, breathless, within the circle of his locked arms. 'You had no right to take my things out of my bag!' she yelled at him when she'd got her breath back. 'And if I want a drink or a cigarette, then I'll damn well have one.' She glared up at him, chest heaving, her face flushed with exertion.

There was a tired look around Scott's eyes as he said, 'Can't you see that you're only destroying yourself? The way you're heading you'll either have a nervous breakdown or become an alcoholic in a few months.'

'So what?' Alexa jeered. 'I'll do what I damn well like! Who the hell cares anyway?' she added on a note that was close to despair.

Scott's arms tightened until they hurt. 'I care,' he said roughly.

'You!' She tilted her head to look at him in open disbelief. 'You? Care? Oh, that's funny, that's really funny!' And she began to laugh hysterically.

'Stop it! Alexa, stop it or I'll have to slap you!' His hands moved up to her shoulders and he shook her roughly.

Her high laughter stopped abruptly and she stood trembling until she said with difficulty, 'I'm—I'm all right now. You can let me go.'

He did so slowly, his eyes wary in case she tried to

lash out at him. But Alexa moved away and stood looking at him, her hands clenched tight by her sides. She was calmer now but there was fierce determination in her voice as she said, 'You have no right to stop me doing whatever I want. And if I choose to go to hell in my own way, that's my business.'

A disdainful look came into his eyes, one that she hadn't seen there for quite some time, 'You're taking the coward's way out again, Alexa.'

'Maybe I am,' she answered steadily. 'But have you thought that any other way might be completely unbearable?' A flash of what might have been pain came into Scott's eyes and he opened his mouth to speak, but she went on, 'You can't keep me as a sort of prisoner in the house for ever. Sooner or later I'm going to find some drink.' She turned away and gripped the back of a chair, her knuckles white. 'I—I need a drink to—to keep going.' She gave a brittle kind of laugh. 'Silly, isn't it?'

Scott's mouth twisted. 'No, you don't,' he said roughly, 'because I'm taking you home.'

Turning her head, she frowned in puzzlement. 'Home?'

'Back to England.'

'But—you still have almost a month to do here. How can you . . .'

'I saw my boss this morning and told him that I wanted to go back early. Luckily they already have a replacement lined up for me so it didn't set too much of a problem.'

'But I can't let you do that for me. I have no right to.'

'You have every right,' Scott returned brusquely. 'You're my wife.'

Alexa stared into his face for a moment, then looked

away. 'No,' she said brokenly, 'I'm not your wife.'

They were both silent for a long moment, then Scott broke it by saying, 'We can leave here in three days. Will you promise not to drink any more till then?'

She nodded. 'I'll—I'll try. But surely ...' She hesitated. 'I'm quite sure you don't want to go back to England yet. So why don't you just put me on a plane and let me go home alone?'

'I've said I'm taking you back,' he answered shortly. 'I brought you out here and I'll take you home.'

Alexa went about her packing fitfully, taking no real interest in it, having no real interest even in going back to England. When she thought about it at all she supposed Scott was only taking her back early because she had become a liability and he just wanted to get an annulment quickly and be rid of her. The thought hurt, of course, but no more so than his first rejection had. Personally she didn't care where she went. The hurt wasn't going to get any better just because she was in England, but at least if she was free of him and never saw him again, then she might begin to make some semblance of a life for herself. Although any life she could envisage hardly bore thinking about. Even being with him knowing that he didn't want her was better than that.

On their last night in Brazil, they went to the Club with Tony Grant and found all the crowd there, ready to wish them well. Patti Jordan and her husband were there, too, and came over to say goodbye.

'I'm sorry we haven't had time to get to know one another better,' Patti remarked, drawing Alexa to one side as the men talked together. 'I've an idea that we could have been friends. And I would very much like to have seen your orchid paintings.'

'Scott told you about that?' Alexa asked in surprise.

'He told me a great deal about you. In fact, he seldom stopped talking about you. And now that you're going back to England you'll be able to have the honeymoon that he wants so much.'

That remark was puzzling, but Alexa had no time to dwell on it because some other people came up to her, and they left soon after as they had to catch an early morning plane.

The journey home was long and tiring as they had to go via Rio de Janeiro. Alexa tried to sleep on the plane, but kept remembering how she had felt on the flight out to Brazil. Then she had been grieving for Mark, but it was nothing compared to what she felt for Scott. They landed at Heathrow in the early afternoon and walked out of the terminal building to find that it was raining. Not the thick, heavy sheeting rain of Brazil but the soft, fine rain of England that left a smell of washed-cleanness behind it instead of humid dankness.

Scott had arranged to pick up a hired car at the airport and he loaded their cases into the boot while Alexa sat inside out of the rain. He got in beside her and at first it seemed strange and frightening to be driving on the left again. Alexa sat gazing out of the window, realising how familiar Brazil had become but how quickly it would fade. But not all of it, some things would always stay fresh and vivid in her memory. And perhaps, in time, they would just be the good things. Scott drove on and they were several miles into the outskirts of London before she roused herself to ask, 'Where are we going?'

He gave a small smile. 'I wondered when you'd get round to asking me that. I'm taking you to my parents' home.'

Alexa turned her head to stare at his hard profile. 'But why there? Why not to a hotel or something?'

He shrugged. 'It seems as good a place as any.'

His parents lived in Cambridgeshire, not far from the university town, and as they drove northwards, through the broad flat lands of the fens, the rain stopped and the sun broke weakly through the clouds, so that when they turned in at the gates and drove down the gravelled driveway towards the old house, the sun was reflected a thousand times in all the lattice-windows.

Scott had telephoned ahead and his parents knew they were coming. They came out as soon as they heard the car and hurried to greet their elder son, while Alexa tactfully stood back, looking out across the grounds. She had been here before, of course, when she had first become engaged to Mark and he had brought her down to meet his parents, and several times later. The house was early Victorian, built of red-brick that was still mellowing into rose pink, the walls covered with green Virginia creeper that turned to rich copper in the autumn. Alexa had fallen for the house when she first saw it and wished now that Scott hadn't brought her here. She didn't want to be sad in this house, to have the final break happen here.

'My dear child—welcome home.' Scott's mother came to her with a smile and a hug. 'Good heavens, how tired you look. Such a long journey. Come in and have a coffee.'

His father came over to welcome her too, although less effusively. His sons had inherited his eyes, which looked at her so keenly, seeing a great deal.

Mrs Kelsey fussed around her, making her sit in a comfortable chair and put her feet up on a stool.

Alexa laughed rather nervously. 'Oh, please, don't bother. I'm fine, really.'

'Scott said on the phone that you hadn't been

feeling too good, so now that you're here you must have a long rest and get perfectly well again.'

Alexa shot a quick glance at Scott, but he was standing by the window, talking to his father, and he didn't look at her until his mother called him over for coffee.

They talked easily together, the three of them, while Alexa sat back in her chair, sipping the coffee. His parents were telling him all the news, their eyes on him, smiling, greedy to look at him after all the weeks he had been away. And Scott listened with a smile, occasionally making a remark or asking a question, his love for them showing in his voice and in his face. Oh God, what she wouldn't give to have him look at her like that, speak to her like that. Just once. Only once. As if her thought had communicated itself to him, Scott looked at her suddenly, his eyes meeting hers. For that brief second his face looked bleak and vulnerable, but then his expression changed, became a frozen mask, before he turned back to his parents.

After they had had coffee, Mrs Kelsey led them upstairs. 'I've put you in the big guest room,' she told them. 'It's at the front and gets the sun in the morning,' she explained to Alexa.

'Thank you, but I—er . . .'

Scott came to her rescue. 'Alexa hasn't been sleeping very well since she's been ill,' he said easily. 'I think it would be better if we had separate rooms, so I'll go in my old room, shall I? It's available, I take it?'

'Why, yes, of course. I'll tell Mrs Stevens to make the bed up.'

She hurried away, and Alexa found that she was trembling.

'Relax,' Scott warned her. He picked up her cases and carried them into the room. 'Perhaps you'd better try to have a rest before you unpack.'

'Is there any point in unpacking? I mean, I don't know how long you want me to stay here.'

He straightened up and turned towards her. 'What do you mean?'

'Well, I—I expect you'll want me to go as soon as you apply for the annulment.'

'We'll talk about that later,' he answered harshly. 'There's plenty of time. Unpack your things and try to have a rest before dinner.'

Alexa started to unpack, but halfway through felt so tired that she lay down on the big bed and fell into a deep sleep. She woke feeling much better, but her face was still pale and there were dark shadows around her eyes when she came down to dinner. Scott's parents greeted her kindly enough, but she shot a quick look at Scott across the room, wondering how much he had told them, whether they now knew the truth. During the meal Scott kept the conversational ball rolling over general topics, often talking about Brazil and drawing her into it with a question or to ask an opinion. She spoke rather reluctantly, feeling like an intruder at the family table. She didn't eat very much either, and she drank only sparingly of the wine.

Afterwards, she helped Mrs Kelsey to carry the dishes through to the kitchen and stack them in the dishwasher.

'Did you see a doctor while you were in Brazil, Alexa?' the older woman asked her.

She flushed and shook her head. 'No, it was just—just that the climate didn't suit me.'

'Oh, I see. Nothing serious, then?'

'No.'

'Oh. Good. I phoned Mark and Elaine to let them know you were coming home, by the way. They're longing to see you. I expect they'll be down at the weekend.' Mrs Kelsey smiled. 'How lovely! I shall have all my family together for the very first time. Both of my great big sons, and both my lovely daughters-in-law!'

Alexa's face tightened and she blinked hard. 'Would—would you excuse me? I'm afraid I still feel terribly tired. I expect it's jet-lag or something.'

'Yes, of course, dear. You go on up and I'll send Scott with a hot milk drink for you.'

'No. No, I don't want anything. Would you say goodnight to them for me, please?' And she hurried from the room.

They let her sleep as long as she liked the next day and when she awoke Alexa's body clock was so out of sync that she had no idea whether it was morning or afternoon. Going to the window, she looked out over the lawns and flower beds that surrounded the house. The sun was out and the flowers in the long borders looked gently colourful; English flowers; not the exotic, brilliant blooms of Brazil. Suddenly she was glad to be home where she belonged. She dressed and went downstairs, to see by the grandfather clock in the hall that it was almost one. Mr Kelsey came out of his study as she stood there, adjusting her watch.

'Hallo, there. Feeling any better?'

'Yes, thank you.'

'Good. You're just in time for lunch. We're having it outside in the garden today.'

He led the way to a patio that had been built on to the back of the house where Scott and his mother were already waiting.

'Sleep well?' Scott come over to her and kissed her lightly on the cheek. Alexa looked at him with a puzzled frown, wondering why he was keeping up the pretence instead of taking his parents into his confidence.

She thought he might explain when he asked her to go for a walk with him after lunch, but he seemed disinclined to open the subject, walking along with a brooding look on his face, his hands thrust in his pockets. So at length she asked him herself.

He shrugged. 'There's no point in worrying them until the time comes.'

'But surely you want to get the marriage annulled as soon as possible?'

'Do you?' He didn't look at her.

Alexa closed her eyes in pain, then said heavily, 'Yes, of course.'

They walked on for quite a few yards before Scott said, 'It isn't as easy as that. An annulment isn't open to us any more.'

'Why not?' She stopped and turned to face him.

'Because we don't have the grounds. The marriage has been consummated.'

'Oh!' Alexa's face flamed. 'So what do we have to do?'

'Get a divorce, I suppose.'

'But that takes time, doesn't it?'

'Yes. We wouldn't be free for a couple of years.'

'I see.' She walked over to a nearby gate and rested her arms on the top bar. 'Couldn't we pretend that we hadn't . . . that we still had the grounds? After all, no one's to know.'

'Are you so eager to be rid of me that you'd commit perjury in court?' Scott demanded harshly.

She turned to stare at him, taken aback by his fierceness, then shook her head dumbly.

'There's something else I have to ask you,' Scott said slowly. 'Are you—pregnant?'

Her face very white, Alexa again shook her head.

'Could you be?'

'No.'

After that they didn't speak for several minutes. Staring out over the green meadows, Alexa gathered her courage and at last looked towards him. 'I—I just wanted to say something before we—before we split up. I never thanked you for saving my life that time.' He made an abrupt, negative gesture, but she went on, 'I'm very grateful, and I'm grateful to you for looking after me the way you did. I know that I've been a nuisance and a liability, and that having to marry me has ruined a good bit of your life, especially now that we'll have to get a divorce.' Her voice faltered. 'I'm terribly sorry about that. More sorry than I can say.'

He turned on her suddenly. 'Don't ever say that,' he said forcefully. 'Do you hear me? Don't ever say you're sorry.' For a moment it seemed as if he was about to catch hold of her, but he thrust his hands back into his pockets. 'I wouldn't have done it if I hadn't wanted to. None of it. Do you understand?'

Alexa nodded her head, afraid of his sudden outburst, although she didn't really understand at all.

He moved away. 'We'd better get back to the house. I wanted to tell you that I have to go up to London for a couple of days. I'll be back on Saturday.'

They walked the rest of the way in silence and shortly after they got back he drove away, leaving Alexa to spend the next two days alone with his parents. The time went easily enough; she took long walks in the grounds or helped to weed the flower beds, wanting to make herself useful. The Kelseys were kind to her and didn't ask questions, although Alexa sensed that Mrs Kelsey would have loved to have a long chat and find out how she and Scott had got together and why so quickly. But Mr Kelsey was definitely the master in that household, and if his wife started on any personal topic he subtly and cleverly changed the subject.

Scott came back on Saturday morning, but he hadn't told Alexa that he was travelling down with Mark and Elaine. The two brothers walked into the room together and Alexa's heart missed several beats. They were so alike. And both of them had a place in her heart. She looked at Mark first, able to see him now without any heartache, not even regret, just sweet nostalgia for a love that had passed. Then she looked at Scott, and saw the bleakness in his face, the tired, fed-up look in his eyes. Slowly she got to her feet, wondering if his journey to London had anything to do with the divorce.

Mark came over to give her a hearty kiss. 'Darling, you look wonderful! Welcome to the clan. It was obvious from the start that you'd end up as a Kelsey. You just picked the wrong one to start with, that's all,' he told her with all his old, irrepressible charm.

Alexa smiled at him. 'You're quite right, I did. You were definitely the wrong one for me, Mark.'

She felt Scott look at her quickly, but then Elaine came in and ran to greet her. The family were all together then until it was time to change for dinner in the evening. Alexa thought that perhaps Scott might come and tell her what he'd been doing in London, but he didn't, and she went down to dinner alone, wearing a long white evening dress because they were dressing up tonight. The dress had a halter-neck top and no back, revealing the rich gold of her tan, the swathed skirt swirling about her ankles.

'Wow!' Mark whistled when she came into the room, but her eyes went to Scott wearing a black evening suit that emphasised his dark good looks.

During dinner she sat next to Scott and opposite Mark, who kept asking her lots of questions about Brazil. The table was large and there was plenty of space between them. Their hands only touched accidentally once all evening. After the pudding Mark rose and banged on the table for silence. 'Elaine and I have a very wonderful announcement to make,' he told them. 'We're going to have a baby!'

Immediately there was a babble of delighted questions and congratulations from the prospective grandparents. Alexa began to get to her feet, but found Scott's hand on her arm, his face wary and frowning, and she realised that he was afraid she was going to make a scene. 'It's all right,' she assured him, and stood up, raising her glass. 'I'd like to propose a toast. To the Kelseys. Of all three generations.'

There was general laughter and applause as she drank, then Elaine laughed excitedly and said, 'But you're a Kelsey, too, Alexa.'

'Yes,' Mark agreed. He turned to his brother. 'You're not going to let us get away with this, are you? You and Alexa must start a family soon.'

Alexa flushed, but felt her eyes drawn to Scott's face.

He lifted his glass, his grey eyes holding hers, and said softly, 'Believe me, there's nothing I'd like better.'

Hastily she turned away, her heart doing somersaults. The others laughed, thinking her embarrassed, but Alexa was wondering desperately whether he'd meant it or whether he was still putting on an act for his parents' sake.

It was about two before they finally split up and Alexa went to her room to undress. She did so slowly, remembering that one sentence, and going over and over it again. She put on a black lace nightdress and automatically brushed her long, dark hair. Other things came back: the way he had treated her before they had made love, his declaration in the garden here that everything he'd done, he'd wanted to do. Put all these things together with his icy withdrawal after the night they'd spent together and it just didn't make sense. She'd got to know why he had changed so suddenly. *She just had to know.*

Without stopping to think, she ran out of her room and down the corridor, flinging open the door of his room. He had taken off his jacket and tie but was otherwise fully dressed, leaning against the window embrasure and gazing out into the garden, that bleak look back in his eyes.

As she swept in he straightened up and stared at her, his hands coming out of his pockets. 'Alexa . . .'

He started to say her name, but she pushed the door shut and ran to him, her eyes desperate with appeal. 'I've got to know. You've got to tell me.' She caught hold of his arms, her nails digging in like talons. 'After that night you—you made love to me. Why were you so cold to me? What had I done to make you hate me?'

'Hate you?' His hands came up to cover hers, pull them down. 'Dear God, of course I don't hate you.'

'Then why? Why are you treating me like this?' She gazed up at him pleadingly, tears gathering in her eyes.

Putting a hand on either side of her head, Scott said urgently, 'When I woke that morning you were still asleep. I got up and went outside, but when I came back you were . . .,' he paused, his mouth twisting in pain, 'you were awake. You were lying in bed sobbing as if your heart would break. I thought you were crying because of what had happened between us.

Because you realised it was I who had made love to you and not Mark. I thought you'd deluded yourself into thinking it was him again, you see. Especially after you lied and said you'd been to bed with him. I thought you were still in love with him and that going to bed with me was the worst thing that could have happened to you.'

'Oh, Scott!' She gazed at him in growing wonder. 'Of course I knew it was you. Didn't I tell you so? I'd stopped loving Mark some time before that and I *wanted* you to make love to me. Wanted it very much.'

'But why were you crying?'

She laughed tremulously. 'Because I was so happy, you big fool! Because I thought you loved me. And sad, too, because I'd been so stupid over Mark, and because we'd wasted so much time. And most of all because I loved you.'

His hands came down on her shoulders and he gripped them tightly. 'What did you say?'

'That I loved you. Very much.'

'Oh God, Alexa,' he breathed. 'If you only knew how long I've waited to hear you say that! I fell for you the day we met, but then I found out about Mark. I was angry then because no man likes being used, especially when his emotions are involved. But I used you in a way too.' She looked at him questioningly and he went on. 'I used your taking those pills as an excuse to take you back to Brazil with me. You see, I hoped even then that one day you'd forget Mark and turn to me. Didn't I tell you that I loved someone who didn't love me in return?'

'Oh, my dear!' Her hand came up to gently caress his face. 'If only I'd known!'

He grinned suddenly. 'I did tell you. When we were

making love, but you were a bit preoccupied at the time and didn't hear.' His face shadowed again. 'I was going to tell you properly when you woke up, but then I saw you crying.'

'Oh, Scott!' Her arms went round his waist and they clung to each other tightly. 'We've been such fools. Such stupid . . .' But her words were lost as his mouth came down on hers with a fierce hunger, a hunger of pain and disappointment that could only be assuaged in the certainty of love.

It was some time before either of them had breath for anything but hot, rapturous kisses, but then Alexa pulled a little away from him and said teasingly, 'Are we still going ahead with that divorce?'

'We most certainly are not,' he returned, firmly pulling her back in his arms.

'Isn't that why you went to London?'

'No, I went to arrange to work over here instead of going abroad again. I was still hoping, you see, that once you'd seen Mark again you might realise it was hopeless and turn to me. Might even find out that you didn't love him any more.'

'I don't. Really I don't.'

'Why did you tell me that you'd slept with him?'

'I don't know—because you kept asking me, I suppose, and it made me angry. It seemed to matter so much to you. Why did it?'

'I think because quite early on you compared me to Mark as a lover, and I had this feeling that if you'd slept with him you'd never get over him and give yourself to me completely.'

'But I have, Scott, I swear it!'

'When we came in the door,' Scott said slowly, 'you looked at him first, for a long time.'

'Yes,' Alexa acknowledged. 'I can't really explain it,

but I was sort of saying goodbye.'

'But you said once that he would always be in your heart.'

'Yes, he will. A girl's first love always has the first place in her heart. But you, my dearest love, will always have the last.'

He laughed then, a deep laugh of happiness and contentment. Swinging her up into his arms, he carried her over to the door and opened it.

'Where are we going?' Alexa demanded in astonishment.

'To your room.'

'But . . . Oh!' She broke off as she saw Mark and Mr Kelsey at the top of the stairs, their eyebrows raised in astonishment.

'Goodnight, Father. Mark,' Scott said quite calmly as he passed them.

Alexa peeped over his shoulder and saw that the two men both had huge grins on their faces.

'What was wrong with your room?' she demanded.

'The bed's too small. It cramps my style.'

'I didn't notice it doing that before,' she answered pertly.

He carried her into her room and shouldered the door shut. 'But you will, Mrs Kelsey. You most definitely will!'